LAIKA

NICK ABADZIS

Color by Hilary Sycamore

:01
First Second
NEW YORK & LONDON

CHAPTER 1

I am a man of destiny ... I will not die ...

I am a man of destiny ... I will not die ...

... I am a man of destiny ...
... I will not die ...

I am a man of destiny ...

RRRMM
... I will not –

STOP! PLEASE!

Thank you! Thank you!
TSSS

Please ... I need to get to Magadan.
All right.

What can you pay me?

I – I have no money.

Give me your coat and I'll take you.

Please ... I **need** my coat. Without it, I'll freeze to death.

As I see it, you've got no choice.
Anyway, you'll be **warm** in here.

If I give you my coat, I'll still die of cold when you let me off in Magadan.

I have a better chance if I keep the coat and just keep walking.

No. If you do that, you'll *definitely* die.
And you won't get the coat.

All right, you've got a point. What else have you got?

What about this sweater? It's old but thick and warm.

Deal. Let's go.

What's your name, friend, and why are they letting you walk out of the gulag?
Korolev.
KOFF

I've been recalled to Moscow. My case is being reinvestigated.
KOFF
Lucky.

For most, there's only *one* way out of the Kolyma gulags.
I know.
KOFF

KOFF
KOFFF
HAAAACK
KOFF
Easy, friend. That's a bad cough.

Yes.
I am a man of destiny. I will not die
What?
Nothing ...
... just a maxim of mine. I keep repeating it. It's kept me going.
Hey, friend ... wake up!
You fell asleep.
I turn off here. It's a short walk to Magadan.
Bear left for the port. If you're lucky, the last ship of the season won't have sailed yet.
Thank you.
Hey, friend – comrade – some advice ...
Eat soon. Find shelter. Otherwise, coat or no coat, you won't last.
I am a man of destiny ... I will not die ... I am a man of destiny ...

I am a ...

... will not ...

Will not ...

Thank God ...

Don't think that I haven't noticed you, my friend ...
Man of destiny

... looking down on me ...
Will not die

Are you mocking me? Is that it?
Man of destiny

You look so close.
Close enough ...
... to touch ...
Or you're **helping** me? A guardian angel, perhaps? ...
... Lighting my way ...
... through this frozen, silent world ...
Not silent ...
Not a delusion ...?
How welcome is such a familiar sound ...
Find shelter. Otherwise, coat or no coat ...
Follow it, Sergei Pavlovich ...
It'll find you somewhere **warm**.

... like an army barracks.
I am a man of destiny ...
... Warm bread?
Is this a joke?
... A kind of miracle?

Ah! I see it.
A good guardian angel, yes ...

ZNNNN

ZNNN

Man of Destiny

For God's sake, comrade, come in and shut the door. You're letting in a draft!

Sorry ... **comrade.**

A good guardian angel ... yes!
I am a man of destiny ...
I will not die.
I AM A MAN OF DESTINY!

Tyura-Tam, Kazahkstan, October 4th 1957...
Eighteen years later
I've been waiting for this moment all my life!
Chief Designer! Here it comes again ...

BEEPBEEEEEEEEEPEEEEEEEEPEEP

Ha-haaa! Listen to that, gentlemen ...

That is the sound of the first artificial satellite in orbit around Earth.
We built it ...

IT IS RUSSIAN!

WHOOH!
HURRAY!
YAY!
WHOO!
HOOOOOOO!

Shabarov! Extra rations to celebrate. Dispense one teapot each of extra alcohol to every man on this launch ground!
Immediately, Chief Designer!

And to ***you,*** my friend ... I've not forgotten ***you.***

Hey, Sergei Pavlovich! Ryabikov phoned the Premier. He said Khruschev was **pleased.**

"Pleased"?
Give him a day or so ...

... he'll soon realize the propoganda value of this achievement.

I tell you, Mstislav, this day will go down in history.

Today, the people of the world will stop thinking of themselves as a two-dimensional civilization wrapped around a ball ...

Now, they will begin to look **upward** ...
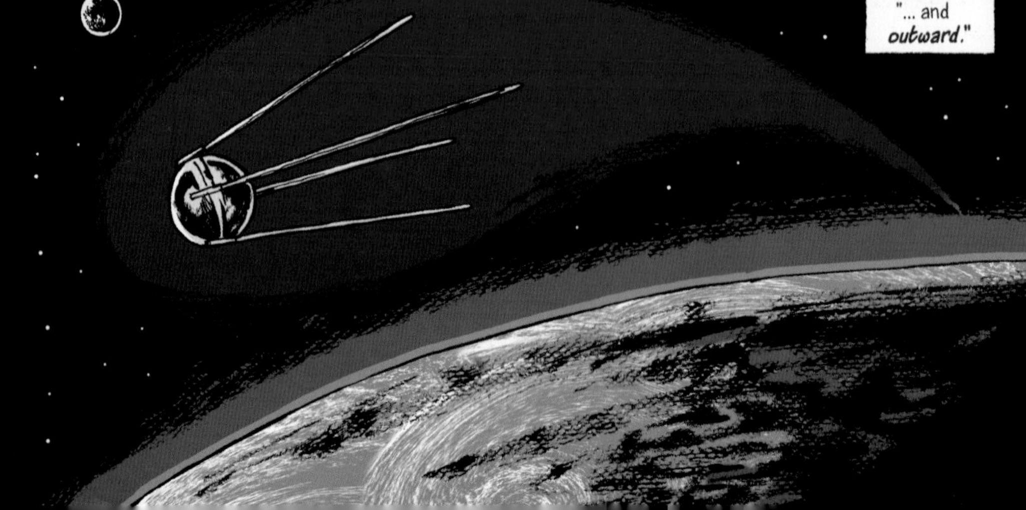
"... and **outward.**"

Moscow, next day:
October 5th, 1957

Welcome back, Sergei Pavlovich!
Congratulations, Chief Designer!
Vasili! Antonina!

These are great days for our little design bureau, my friends! OKB-1 leads the world!
Haha! The whole world is talking about our satellite, Sergei ...
It's gone crazy!

They're calling it Sputnik I. It's all over the front page of Pravda ...
Pravda? Good, good ...

And I have British newspapers, French, German, American ...
Pravda is quoting the congratulations of the USA's Press.

There's a timetable here that shows when the satellite will be visible over Washington DC.
Hahaha!

Incredible! Just imagine Eisenhower, out on his porch, watching a Russian satellite crossing the sky over his precious land!

"Where? Is the sky falling?"
HA-HAA!

Listen, Vasili. It is vital that we don't let this momentum fail.
And ...

Premier Khruschev wants to talk to you.
When?

As soon as possible.
The Council of Chief Designers is meeting with Khruschev's aide tomorrow ...

... But the Premier wants to speak with you today, in private.
Excellent! I knew he'd get it!

Driver, drop these two back at the bureau and then take me straight to the Premier's office.
Yessir.

He's all revved up, Antonina.
Comrade Mishin ...

Is it really true that Chief Designer Korolev was once a prisoner in a gulag?

Yes, it's true. Because of false allegations, of course. He never speaks of it and neither should you.
He loves his country, like any other Russian.

I didn't mean – I just meant to say, how remarkable –
I know.
Ready yourself, because I have a feeling it's not going to stop here.
Comrade Korolev! This is a remarkable achievement.
Oh, I laughed when I thought of all those yankees tuning in their radios to hear the beep-beep of our Sputnik ...
So ingenious.
Thank you, Premier.

But what I want to know is, how soon can you launch another one?
Another ...?

Well, we're working on a **second** orbital vehicle right now.

Can it be launched in time for the 40th anniversary of the Revolution on November 7th?
A month?
Uhh ... well ...
That's a very **tight** deadline!

Listen to me, Sergei Pavlovich. I want to **grind** the USA's **face** into this ...

...Those arrogant, strutting **bastards!**

Imagine what it's like for them to know there's a piece of **Soviet hardware** circling the Earth, above their heads!

Eisenhower must be waking up at night in a cold sweat!
Ha ha.

Sputnik I demonstrates the **superiority** of our socialist system. Which is why we need to launch a second one to highlight our **success**.

Can you do it?
...
Of course, Premier.

Good. I want another coup like this one, Korolev ...

Let's show the whole world the advantages of socialism!

What can be done to make a second Sputnik different to the first?
One possible step would be to send a biological organism up to see if it can survive –

Can you put a man up there?
A man ...!

Premier Khruschev, with your help, one day I hope to see our fellow Russians in orbit, perhaps even walking on the moon!
Indeed ...?

But for Sputnik II – well, it's a little premature to consider a manned flight. Maybe in a year or two.

But I do have another idea ...

Ha haaa!
I knew you would!

God's Teeth!
A MONTH?!

I know, I know.
It's a crazy deadline.
Crazy? It's impossible!
And I just sent most of our staff on vacation!
Call them back.
Vasili, we have the blessing of the Premier.
He told me that we must make this date "without fail."
We're committed to it?
Sergei Pavlovich – what have you done?
We'll never have 'Object D' ready in time!
Forget 'Object D'! We'll build a completely new spacecraft ...
We'll make it as simple as possible.
Simple! But –
Vasili, three months ago, we couldn't even get our R-7 rocket to fly.

Yesterday, it launched Sputnik I!
True ...

We **can** do this.
We **must**.
OKB-1 is the best design and engineering bureau in Russia. Imagine the kudos **another** launch will bring us!

This is only the first step to realizing our **dream** – putting Russians on the Moon!

A **month!** Maybe it can be done ...
That's the spirit. It's a **challenge!**

Now recall Chertok and the others. We have work to do.

CHAPTER 2

Moscow

Three years earlier

This is *intolerable*, Tatiana. A *disaster!*

How, Madam?
I don't care!
Drown them if you have to!
Seven! That's a lot of babies.
We'll have to wait 'til their eyes are open before we part them from you.
Don't worry. We'll find them all good homes, I promise.

I won't have mongrels in this house!
There, there. Don't listen to the old bat. Had a difficult time, didn't you, girl?
Mew
Look at you! ...
You're ready to go *now!* Well, calm down, little one ...
KUDRYAVKA.

... I have to find someone who'll have you, first.

Look at *this!*
Little Curly! Kudryavka!

Щенки!

Mama, can we keep Kudryavka? You ***said*** she was special!

Sigh

No. We already have a dog and a cat.

I have too many mouths to feed as it is, Tatiana. Why would I want another?

Take my advice and dump them.
Throw them in the river.

A ***puppy?*** God, ***no!***
He already feeds all the filthy strays as it is!
Only one or two ...!

We don't need any more dogs!
All right. I understand.
Bleeding-heart ***madwoman.***
What are you looking at? Get back to work!

Seven puppies that no one wants ...

!
Liliana! Come here!

Hello, Mama. Back from market?
Yes. And I have a job for you. Show this to your friends ...

Ask which of them would like a sweet little puppy. I'll be back with them when school finishes.
Here's my mama!
Puppies!
I want one!

Who wants a puppy, then?
I've wrapped them in blankets ...
Me!
Me!

There ...! Take good care of them!

One left: Kudryavka.
Oh, Mama, let's keep her!

Well ...

Tatiana!
Katya! How are you?...

You look so tired!
It's Mikhail. he's playing up again.

He's always polite to me, dear cousin.
He's insolent, lazy and destructive. I don't know what to do with him.

Well, what does his father say?

WRF

Er – perhaps Mikhail would like a pet? Meet Kudryavka ...
A puppy?

A gentle, special dog. If Mikhail learned to care for her, perhaps his behavior would improve.
I-
OW!

LILIANA!
He started it! He pulled my hair and he keeps saying dirty things – I hate him!

I've had enough of you, young man!

YOU SEE THIS?
You're going to learn some responsibility. THIS IS YOUR DOG!

But I don't –
SHUT UP! It's YOURS! If you don't feed it, it STARVES!
I-

But –
Thank you, Tatiana.
W-
Come on, you – HOME.

MARCH!

You kept that drawing?
Of course.

It's Kudryavka, isn't it?

I suppose it is.
I don't want to forget her.

She'll only be living down the road.

And we'll put this drawing by your bed.

I wish we could've kept her.

I know, I know ...

A dog?
A puppy.

Tatiana suggested that obliging our son to look after it might teach him some responsibility.
Hm. Your cousin is a silly, soft-hearted cow.

Perhaps. But her children are well-behaved.
You yourself have noted what good socialists they are.

Very well.
We'll try it out.

Thank you.

MIKHAIL! Come here, boy.

Father ...
I have agreed that you are to care for this dog.

Father, I don't want it! Please -
If it gets out of line, you will be responsible.

But -

It's been decided.
That is final.

Am I making myself clear?
Yes, Father.

Hm. Good.
Now get out of my sight and let me finish my dinner in peace.

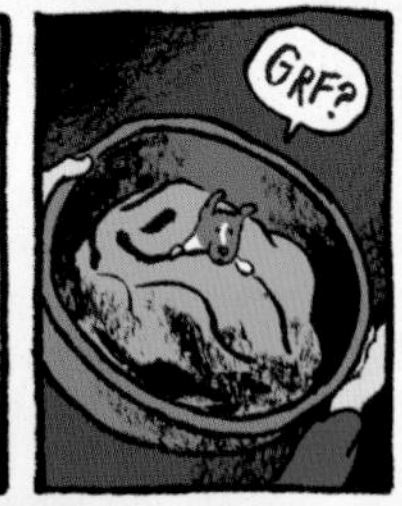
GRF?

WF?

No ... no, **please** ...
I'm no traitor!

I'M INNOCENT!

Sergei, wake up!
Wha-?

You were having a bad dream.
... A bad dream!

What was it?
Nothing.
A memory, that's all.

Go back to sleep, my love.
Mm. You, too.

"A memory."
... A *shadow.*

Mikhail!

Mikhail ...
Dinner's ready.

Have you done your chores?
Yeah, yeah.

Did you polish your father's boots? You know he has the night shift.
Yesss.

There'll be hell to pay if you haven't.
Oh, don't be so boring, Mother.

Have you fed that dog?
WHINE
You're lucky it's so patient. It barely ever whines ...

Aren't you going to let it out of the cupboard?

No.
Oh, don't be ridiculous.

YIP

How long have you had it?
Weeks now and you've shown no interest ...

I NEVER ASKED FOR THE DOG.

Who's shouting? There'll be no shouting in this house unless it's by *me*.

Understand?

Here's your breakfast, dear.

What's this mutt sniffing around for?

Mikhail needs to give it some scraps.

But there are no scraps. I'll have to give it some of my food ...

I don't want it getting underfoot and bothering me with its appetite.
Deal with it.

And make sure you keep it quiet. I don't want it waking me up early.
Yes, Father.

You'll feel my belt if it does, boy.
Yes, Father.

I'm off, now.
Have a good shift, dear.
I will.
Boy! Behave yourself!
Yes, Father.

SLAM

RF?

Go away.

GO AWAY!

YIPE

WF?

skritch
skritch
skritch

SHOO! Go find your master.

...And get me some potatoes.

Yes, Mama.

!

ARF! ARF! ARF!

MMMF
ARF! ARF!

Haha! Hey, Mikhail, who's your little friend?
HA HA HA!
HAHA
HAHA!

MAKE FUN OF ME, YOU BASTARDS...?!
I'LL KILL YOU!

Calm, down, pal!
Take it easy, Mikhail!
What's up with him?
GET OFF ME!

Mikhail, we're not going to play with you if you're going to keep going off like that.
You need to cool off.
Zhopa!
Sobakin sin!

RRUF?
...Still here?
Don't you get it? I don't *want* you. Get lost!

GO ON!

Shame on you, Mikhail Korovin, for treating that puppy the way you do. She's a special dog. All she needs is a little love and affection.

NOBODY LOVES *ME!* WHY SHOULD *I* LOVE THE DOG?!

?

Mikhail, where are you going?
It's late!

I'm taking the dog for a walk.

Nice to see he's taking an interest at last.

YIPE
PLOSH

Z

Z...

?

GRRRR

GRRRR

GRRR!

RAAAAH!

Damned dog! My blankets are damp enough without you pissing all over them!

Katya! Hello!
Tatiana.
How is the little dog I gave Mikhail? Liliana said he was having, er ... problems ...
If it's not working out, I'd take her back.
I don't know how it is. It ran off.
She ran off?!
Mikhail took it for a walk and it ran off.
It was only a dog, Tatiana.
Nooooo!
Stupid, mean boy!
She loved him!
Darling, the streets are full of strays. Not everyone cares for animals like you and I.
She's special. She's run off to find her destiny, that's all.
Close your eyes. Let's imagine where she is ...
If she could talk, what would you ask her?
Are you all right, Kudryavka?
"I'm fine, Liliana."
Where are you?
"Somewhere safe. Don't worry about me."
But I do.
"You mustn't. I'll come back and talk to you tomorrow."
Good.
Kudryavka, can I talk to you anytime?
"Anytime."
As long as it takes for you to forget, Liliana.
You were a special dog. I should've kept you.

Bastards!

Have you seen this?
More hoops for us to jump through ...

More uphill battles ...

More explanations required for moronic military minds!
Sergei! **Calm down!**

Sometimes I feel like giving up.
No, you don't. Besides, no one can do what you do.

That's it? No one else can deal with our esteemed superiors, so **I** am **fated** to?

What are you doing?
Going for a walk.

I need to **think.**
In this? You'll **freeze!**

No, I won't.

I've survived **far** colder.

SQUEEEE

SQUEEE
PLAF

My daughter still worries about you, Kudryavka.
Poor child. She looks at her own dog and thinks of *you*, too.
Still, after all this time, she thinks of you.
And I suppose I do, too.
You're probably out there somewhere, free ...
Maybe you have new friends, new family, now ...
We mustn't worry.
That's a good maxim. I'll keep repeating it to myself.
Because you should never look back.
Don't worry ...
Don't worry.

New friends, new family.
Don't worry ...

WF!
?

Gertruda! Here, girl!

Look what I've got for you.
Good girl.

Viktor, how many times must I tell you?

Don't feed the strays. You'll encourage them.
I only feed the ones I like. Besides ...

...this one's no ordinary stray. She doesn't run with the pack.

That's how she always avoids the dogcatcher.
Clever, you see.

Hello, who's this?
You've brought a friend.

So, you're not a complete loner.
How about that.

You old fool, Viktor.
They're just **dogs**.

Clever dogs, though. Right, Gertruda?

Hmm.

OK, here's something for you too, Curly Tail.
Now get going ...

...before you get me into trouble.

Viktor ...

What did I tell you?

Someone call the dogcatchers! This place is overrun with strays!
Already done!

Don't worry ...

There's two!
Wait, Georgi –

Georgi!
Come back, you idiot!

Never bloody listens. He'll never catch those two.
Why not?

They're not with the pack.
Easier pickings **inside** the marketplace. Come on.

Observe ...
Here, boy!
Nice food!

YIPE!
THWAP!

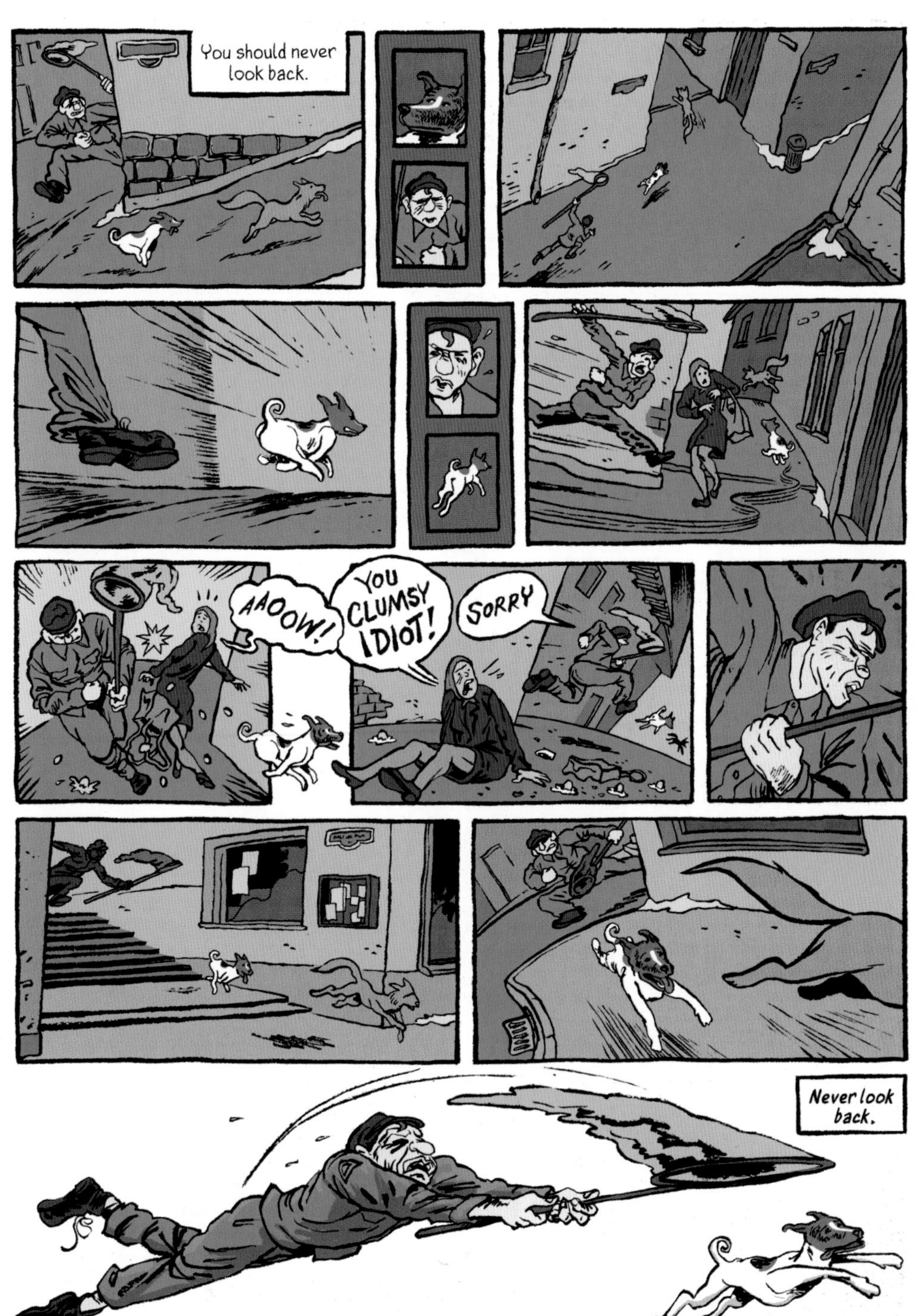
You should never look back.
AAOOW!!
YOU CLUMSY IDIOT!
SORRY
Never look back.

AAAOOW!
OOOHHHhhh...
Filthy mutts.
New friends, new family ...
Don't worry.
WUF?
ROF!
Never look back.
Although, those you leave behind ...
RUF!
ROF!
WOF!
WOF
... will still think of you.

We do still think of you.
We still think of you.
Look, Kudryavka ... you can see the whole world from up here!
Isn't it beautiful?
We're up so high, we could be flying!

Mama ...?

Mama, I had a strange dream.

Tell me.
I dreamed that Kudryavka was flying, and she came to see me.

Flying?
It was horrible to wake up because then she was gone again.

Hmmm. Was she happy in this dream?
Yes!

Well, there, don't you see? Isn't that good?

She must've been trying to tell you that you shouldn't worry.

Hush now, child ...

Try to sleep.
Yes, Mama.

A flying dog ...!
That child ...!

Ah, I love spring!
Best time of year ...

All the pretty flowers come out!
There are two.

Where?

There.

What, the *strays?*
For God's sake, Georgi ...

We've nearly reached the shelter's quota already this month.

Let's not overstretch ourselves.
If you keep talking that way, I'll report you to the local party committee secretary for desertion of duty.

Now, now, calm down. You're new in the job and Piotr's trying to give you the benefit of his experience.
I don't believe it!

It's *them:* the ones I chased from the market that day.
I'm *sure* of it.

Ha! No good – they've seen you, Georgi.

I'm telling you, that scruffy old one's got a sixth sense. You'll **never** catch her.

Piotr's been trying for years.
That's right.

WELL, MAYBE HE HASN'T BEEN TRYING HARD ENOUGH!

I'm the best dogcatcher in Moscow and I'm your senior.

You need to pay attention.
Like, right now. Look ...

HA HA HA HA HA HA!

Come on, Georgi. Let's go find some other stupid mutts.

Never look back.

Academy of Sciences, Moscow
Meeting of the Space Commissioners
Spring, 1956

Congratulations, my dear Sergei Pavlovich.

I never could have done it without your support, my friends.
And I never thought our informal meetings of like minds would lead to something like *this.*
No, Sergei Pavlovich ...
You brought the Premier *and* the Military around.

You made this happen.

Gentlemen – we have permission to *build a satellite.* We have the go-ahead for a *Soviet space program!*

Sergei ... are you all right?

What?
Oh, yes.
We're **safe** for a little while, Vasili Pavlovich.

We're no longer **mavericks.**
For a little while.

So, where's our friend Georgi this morning?
Said he'd meet us around noon. Said he had something to do first ...

Zhopa! That boy ...
I know, I know.

VIKTOR!

VIKTOR!

What are you doing here? Have you forgotten your check-up?

I ... check-up?
For crying out loud, Viktor, are you going soft in the head?

I -
Are you looking for your favorite customers? ... That pretty girl?

Or are you looking for those filthy scavengers? Which is it?

You need to think about what's important.
Because, if you drop dead ...

... and I'm left to look after this stall ...

I WON'T BE THANKING YOU!

You have just enough time to get to the clinic.
All right, woman. Don't start!

Check-up?
?!?

Easy, when you know how.
Now, if we're patient ...

... they'll come.

Aha!

Viktor's not here today. But looky here ...
Look what *I've* got for you!

That's it. Come on!
Come closer...

GRRRRRR

SNF

GRRRRRR

YIPE
YEAH!
WOW-OW-WOW!
YELP
What's that?
It sounds like a -
IN THERE, YOU
WOW-OW-OW
Now for -
RRRRR
YAAAAAAAAH
Mama, I can't -
YIPE
AAAAH!
Come here, you -

Mama
YIIIIII
YIIIIIIII
WOWOOOOOOOOOOOOOOOOOOOOOOO

OWOOOOOOoo

But I think it was a-
It could have been-
We have to go NOW.

ALL RIGHT, NOTHING TO SEE HERE!
PLEASE MOVE ALONG!

You asked for my help to catch these nuisance mongrels.

Instead, you cause a *public spectacle?* Clean up that mess and get out of here.

And don't ever let me see your face here again.
Yes, Ma'am.

Filthy mutts.
But I got you. I *got* you.

PLOSH

Hey, you two! Look what I've got!

See? The one you said I'd never catch.
No ...

We said you'd never catch the **scruffy old one.**

And you didn't, did you?

What's that all over your leg? Your pants are torn. Is it your blood, or the animal's?

I – it – **dammit**, it was only a dog!

You imbecile, Georgi. We're only supposed to **catch** them.
Get in the van, Georgi, and stay there.

I -
One more word out of you and I'll **report** you.

I'll report you for breaking procedure, for unnecessary and malicious cruelty and for ignoring **direct** instructions from your superior.

NOW GET IN THE VAN.

As for you, sweetie - my, you look like you've been through the wars.

Unfortunately, the shelter's overflowing, so you'll have to be put down.
No ...

... we'll take this one to Yazdovsky.

The Air Force chap?
They always need dogs. This poor thing will be well treated there.

CHAPTER 3

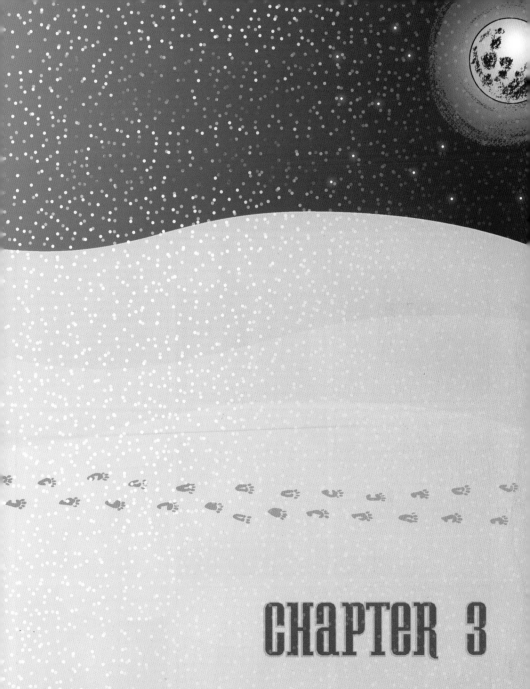

Moscow, Summer, 1956
The Institute of Aviation Medicine: IMBP

Hello. Are you Piotr?
Yeah. Dr. Yazdovsky isn't around?

He's unavailable. He sent me instead. Dr. Oleg Gazenko, at your service.
Good to meet you, Doc.

What do you have for us today, then?
This little one ...

We call her "Zhuchka."
"Little bug?"

Hello, Zhuchka.
She seems very docile.

She's a sweetheart, but I think she's had a hard life.
You can have her for the usual price.

Light fur, even temperament ... what breed?
Part Samoyed, part Terrier ... who knows?

Actually, I'm new in this department and don't usually have much to do with, er ... canine selection.

But she seems perfect. We'll take her.

Dr. Yazdovsky? Uh, Vladimir Ivanovitch?
Ah, Petra. Where's Dr. Yazdovsky?
He's been interviewing candidates for the new assistant post. He might be down in the kennels.
I'm on my way there anyway. Thanks.
Mmhmm.
RF!
Ah! So you *do* talk!
Well, let's introduce you to some new friends.
Vladimir?
Oh!
... Hello!
Oleg Georgivitch!
Dr. Oleg Gazenko ...
May I present comrade Yelena Alexandrovna Dubrovsky.
She's to be our new assistant for dog-training sessions, and here in the kennels, too. She'll be overseeing our other two dog handlers, Konstantin and Yakov.
... Pleased to meet you.

Dr. Gazenko, I'm so pleased we'll be working together.

You've been told of our work here?
I – er, yes, of course.

Yelena is aware that our endeavors here are top-secret and that she'll be bound by all the usual restrictions.

I've filled her in on the broad strokes only.
I see.

Dr. Yazdovsky tells me that, in the short time you've been working for him, you've distinguished yourself in several areas – including that of temporary dog-handler!

I – yes, a strictly unofficial arrangement, to be sure. The dogs –
ROF!

ARF! ARF!
WOOF!
ROWF!
OWF!
WROOF!
WOF
YAP
RARF!
One pipes up and it's a dog chorus!
It's the welcoming committee.

Whenever there's someone new ...

... they're all very curious.
Who's this, then?

Our newest recruit.

Hm. Bit shy.
May I...?

Please!
Come on, let's have a look at you.

What's his name?

Her name. It's a *she.*

All our dogs are female.

Oh?
Makes for more easily maintained sanitation equipment in confined spaces on, uh, *special test flights.*

The dogcatcher called her Zhuchka.
Psst... Zhuchka!

Come on, girl!

Well, hello!

My, my ...

... would you look at that tail!

You're not a **Zhuchka**, a **bug** ...
That's the curliest tail I've ever seen.
So she's a **Curly** ...

... a **Little Curly**, then? **Kudryavka?**

Um, yes. Perfect.
It sounds right.

She **likes** you.
Yes. Dogs **talk** to me!
Well, gentlemen ...

If I'm going to care for these dogs, perhaps I'd better find Kudryavka a place to sleep.
?
You're starting already?

Well, yes.
There's no time like the present, is there?

Excellent! It's settled, then.
Indeed. I, and the department, look forward to working with you, Comrade Dubrovsky.

And I with all of you, Dr. Gazenko.
WOF

Quite a beauty, eh?

Lovely little dog.
No, I meant –

Ah.
I've put your nose out of joint.

I installed a new assistant without giving you or the other physicians in our little team a chance to meet her first.

Or any of the other candidates for that matter, Sir.
Well, I thought it would save time.

And I certainly wouldn't have installed her in the post until I was sure you liked her.

And you did. As will the others, I'm sure.
Yes, Sir.
I expect you'd like me to explain the details of the job to her?

As the newest boy, it's your duty.
Besides, Oleg Georgivitch ...

... you're so much better at that sort of thing than the rest of us.
Thank you, Sir.

But look ... I apologize for dropping her on you like that.

Anyway, Dubrovsky's a clever girl. None of the other applicants came close, from military or civilian backgrounds.
She *is* impressive. And very charming.

Plus she's Major General Pokrovsky's niece.
Ah ... yes.
You **know** about that.

Excellent credentials, I'd say.
She's also a trained nurse with veterinary experience and she's good with little dogs. Perfect for our needs.

Indeed, Sir.
For ***little*** doggies.

So, little limonchik ... what's your story?

Bet you're a pretty dog under that grubby coat. Tomorrow, we'll give you a bath.

Meanwhile, let's find you a nice, big kennel.

What about this one?
This says it belongs to ***Albina*** – but Albina doesn't seem to be here.

It can be your home for now.
GRRR!
ROWRR

Easy! Easy, girl.
Sssh.
GRRRRR

You can trust me. You can trust me.
Good dog. Good dog. Sssh.

Don't like being locked up, eh?
I'm not going to just leave you here.

Good dog. You can trust me.

You and I are going to be good friends.

Good dog. Good girl.

"You can trust me."

I'll see you tomorrow.

"Good dog."

So, they gave you the job!
What are you allowed to tell me about it?
Not much!

Ooh, except I got to rename a dog today.
A dog? !

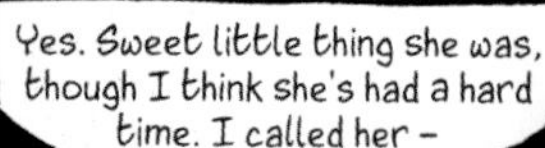
Yes. Sweet little thing she was, though I think she's had a hard time. I called her –

Damn! I can't tell you!

But she seemed sort of familiar and this name popped into my head, so that was that.

Oh dear. You and animals. I hope these bosses of yours know what they're getting themselves into.

They seem very nice. Of course, I'm not allowed to talk about them, either.
Of course.

IMBP – The Institute of Aviation Medicine – Semptember, 1956
Comrade Dubrovsky's met all members of the department now, apart from Academician Blagonravov.

I think she might've found the canine confinement capsule a bit disconcerting at first ...

But once I explained that it was to get the dogs used to the tiny spaces they inhabit aboard test flights, she understood.
Good.

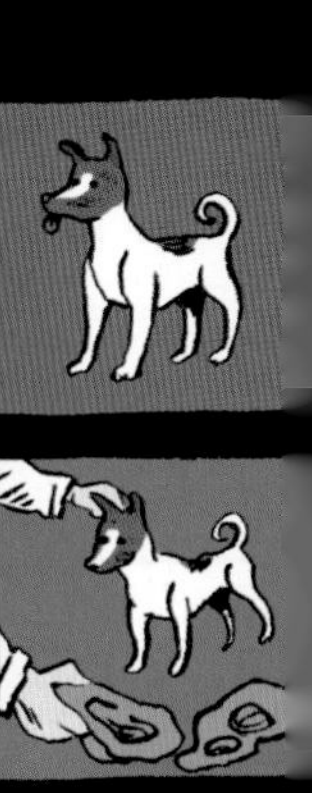

Dr. Gazenko's been showing her the ropes. Ah, there he is now.

Oleg Georgivitch, have you looked in on Yelena today?
On my way there, now. It's Kudryavka's first day at the centrifuge...

?

...might be a bit overwhelming for both of them.
Care to join us?

I have a meeting, but keep me updated.
Indeed.

Oh, and Oleg ...?

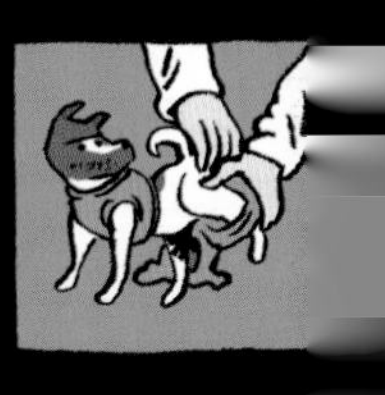

The latest test-flight at Kasputin Yar was successful. The Chief Designer is personally returning both test subjects to us this afternoon.

I'll be ready.

Indeed.

Ah, Dr. Gazenko.
Would you check that I've got this flight suit on properly?

It looks fine.
How's your first week been?

Good. Some of my duties have been – *unexpected*. But ... um, everyone's been very helpful.
... If a little vague?

Yes!...
Do you like dogs, Dr. Gazenko?
It's difficult *not* to, in this place.

But take my advice. Don't get too attached to any of these pooches.
Of course.
Er ... why not?

They go through a lot.
And there have been ...
... *fatalities.*

Fatalities?

Yelena, you've been taken on as an animal technician.
But there's much *more* to this job than that.

I'm sure everyone's been a little **evasive** with you, mentioning **test flights** and all sorts of technical terms, without explaining what they really mean by them.

But if you're to take care of these little canine souls properly ...

... there are a few things you need to know.

What I am about to tell you is a **state secret.**

I've made all my oaths and declarations, Dr. Gazenko.

But whatever I can give, I'll be **proud** to serve my country and the communist party.

Indeed.

Yazdovsky's team – that's us – is engaged in an experimental scientific program to loft animals on vertical rocket flights into the upper atmosphere.

From these test flights, we gather medical data that may one day enable us to prepare a man for flight into space.

These little pooches are our experimental "test pilots."

We loan them, and our expertise, to an external rocket design bureau.
Put her on her leash, will you please?

Our dogs go through a lot. Their training is rigorous.
The training is ...

... difficult.

I believe you've already met Doctors Buylov ...
Popov,
Seryapin
and Parin ...?
... Doctors.
Gentlemen ...

... our newest subject for training – **Kudryavka**.

What is this machine?
A centrifuge. It simulates the g-forces a dog would feel upon rocket launch.

?

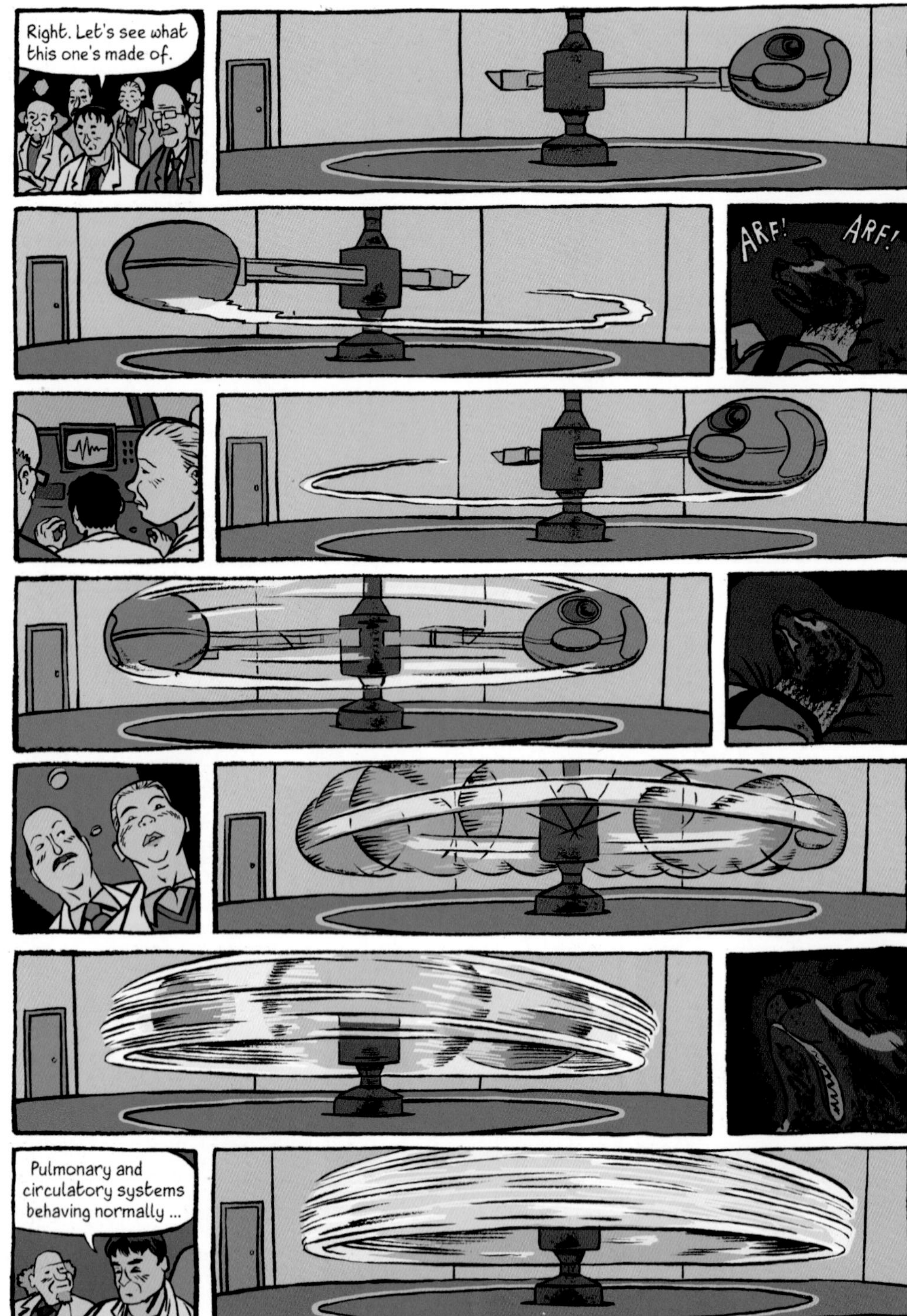
Right. Let's see what this one's made of.
ARF! ARF!
Pulmonary and circulatory systems behaving normally ...

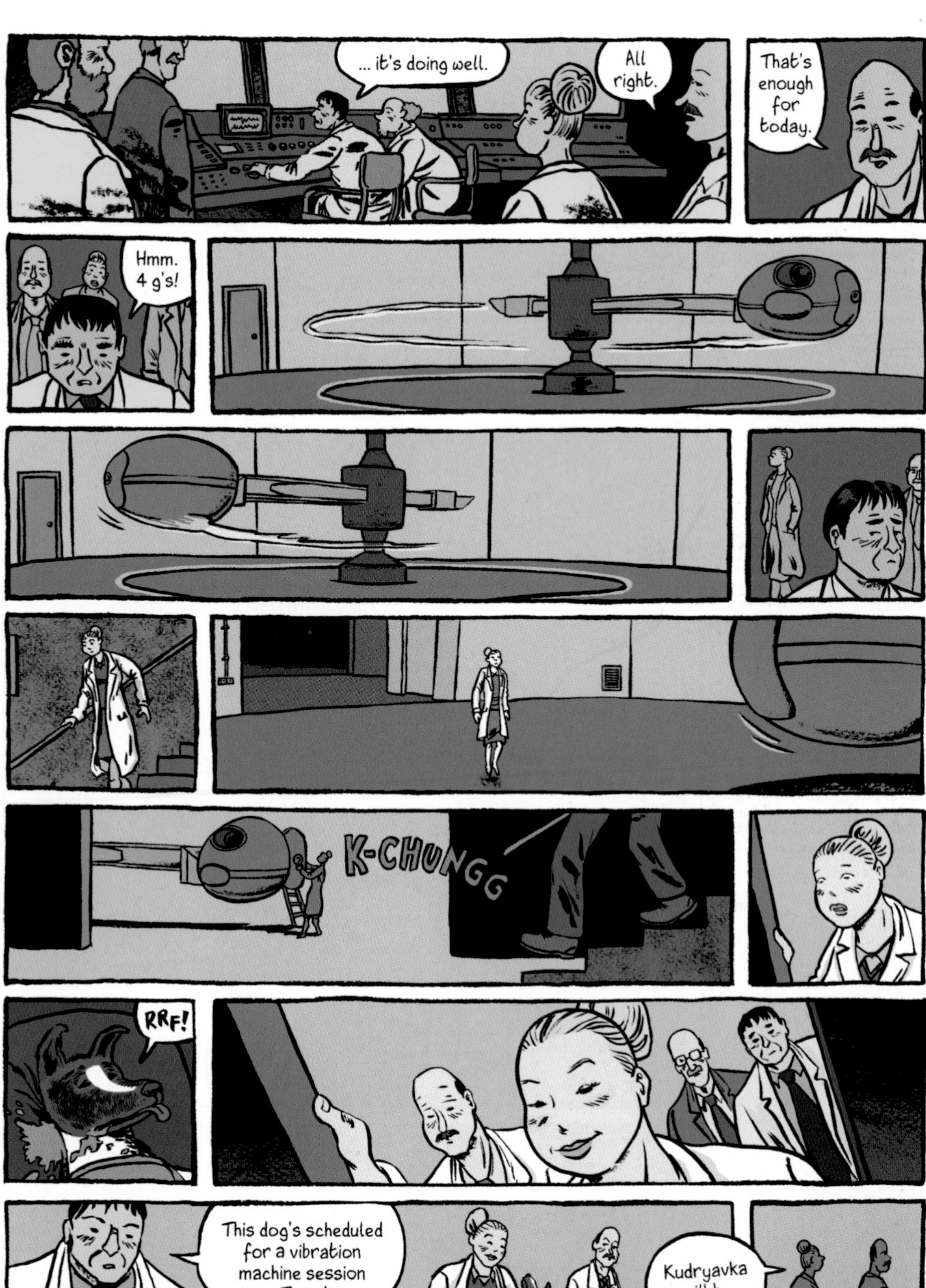
... it's doing well.
All right.
That's enough for today.
Hmm. 4 g's!
K-CHUNGG
RRF!
This dog's scheduled for a vibration machine session on Tuesday.
Kudryavka will be there.

Well, she's regained her appetite.
Soon we'll have to wean her off meat scraps and onto gel food.
Gel food?

Yes. the idea is, gel is easier to eat up in space.

So, you begin to see ... our work here is a lot to get used to.

I'm *up* to it.
It's fantastic. Rocket flights...

It'll take a little while to ***grasp*** it all.

Where is Dr. Yazdovsky?

Ah, Chief Designer. How nice to see you.
I need to debrief Yazdovsky. He isn't in his office.

He's in a meeting. I'll find him for you.

Hello!
I'm Boris!

Uh, hello!
Right. Thanks.

Who is this in Albina's cage?

That's Kudryavka, a new arrival.

And you are ...?
Yelena Alexandrovna Dubrovsky. I'm the new animal technician and assistant to Dr. Yazdovsky's department.

You see, Boris?
Yazdovsky knows what he's doing.
A lovely young lady looking after our dogs.

Our dogs. IMBP loans them to you.

Yelena, we're proud of our brave dogs. They may be small of stature ...
... but they have BIG RUSSIAN HEARTS!
Ah, gentlemen ...

Vladimir!
Sorry to keep you waiting. This way, please.
Oh, and Comrade Dubrovsky ...
Yes?
Give those dogs a treat. They've earned it.
That was ...?
The Chief Designer of rockets.
Ah ...!
He's very charismatic.
Right, I'll leave you to find Albina a home. Got a busy afternoon ...
'Bye.
So, Albina and Kozyavka ... you've touched the edge of space ...
... what's it like out there?

What would you say if you could talk?
"Let me out."
"Let me go."
"What's it like to touch space?"
"Being shot in a tin missile up into the sky?"
"It's noisy, frightening and very dangerous."
"Let me go."
I can't.
That would be a desertion of duty.
Are we friends, Albina?
Mm. Not yet.
What about you, Kudryavka? Friends?
Ah, you're a sweetie ...
... a loyal sweetie.
Good dog.
Yelena?
!
I thought I'd look in on you before going home. It's been a long day for you.
Um, yes – heh.
I was just ... er, talking to the dogs.

Walk you out?
... Certainly.
"Good dog."
"Good dog. You can trust me."
"Trust me."
Don't worry.

Zhukovsky Air Force Base,
35km outside Moscow
October, 1956
Whose idea was this, again?

The physiological data this test will yield will be invaluable.

So it was *your* idea.
It was *Yazdovsky's.*

He's always keen to introduce the latest training methods.
Don't worry, Yelena ...

The dog cabin is padded and pressurized. All Kudryavka will experience is a little confusion and maybe some nausea.
Nausea?
She's used to that – she's been through it all ...

... and now a parabolic flight!

It will briefly produce conditions of **zero G**, during which we'll record any physiological changes.

That's why you scientists like this pooch so much.

Anything you throw at her, she always comes back as patient and loyal as before.
Indeed. "Man's best friend."
WOF!

Yes, I read as much in everyone's reports. If only we knew how she maintains such calm!
Hello, Dr. Yazdovsky.
Grace under fire?

Good dog.
You can trust me.

Don't worry!

?
Never look back
Up so high ...
!
ARF!
ARF!

AWOOOO
oooO(
"You can trust me."
"Good dog!"
OWOOO
AWOOOC
OWOWOWOWOWOWOOO
Each parabola should yield a zero G environment for about 30 seconds ...
Kudryavka's the youngest dog we have, so the results should be –
HERE SHE COMES!

Kudryavka?

Are you all right?

Good dog...

WAKE UP!

YIP!

I've never seen this dog so animated. Isn't she normally quite placid?

She's always happy to see Yelena, Vladimir. Especially after a training session.
ARF!
ARF!
ARF!

Yes, well ...
Don't get too fond of the dogs, will you, Yelena?
No, Doctor.

Exactly as Academician Blagonravov warned, eh, Vladimir Ivanovitch?

Let's collect the data.
Yes, of course.

Psssst!

What *did* Blagonravov say?

Tell you another time!
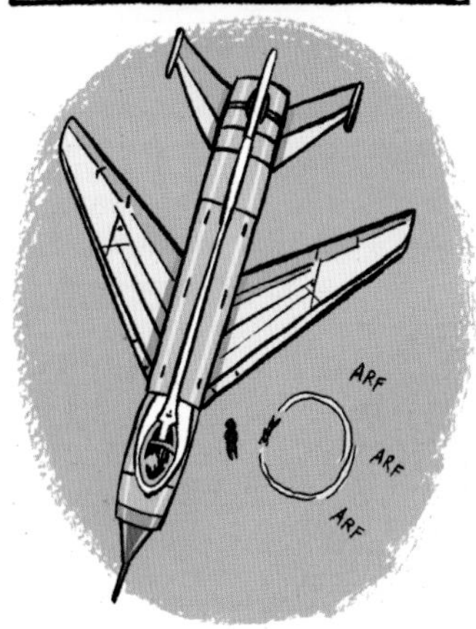
ARF
ARF
ARF

IMBP
One day later
Unusual. Her first reaction seems to be enjoyment ...

...before confusion, or fear.

She was enjoying it! At least, at first.
Fascinating! But why?

No idea. We could send up more dogs and compare results.
There are plans for that.

From a physiological standpoint, I'd say these test results were very positive.

Once again, Kudryavka proves that she's got incredible endurance for a small dog.

Extraordinary ...

Yazdovsky was having trouble interpreting Kudryavka's reactions to zero G.

Really?
He couldn't figure out why she appeared to be enjoying it – at least, early on.

Well, maybe it was like being stuck on one of the rides in Gorky Park for too long.
Ha!

It follows ...

Anyone would get ill and hate it if they stayed on an amusement park ride as long as that.
It's easy to see why she was pleased when it stopped.

You really are becoming a behavioral expert on these dogs.
Thank you. I can usually tell what's bothering them.

That still doesn't really explain her reactions. She's a ***dog!***
What can I tell you? Dogs have emotions. Besides, she's a special dog.

Indeed ...

Members of the Space Medicine Group ...

I'm not at liberty to discuss specifics, but the Chief Designer at the OKB-1 rocket plant tells me that 1957 will see more of his projects in development.

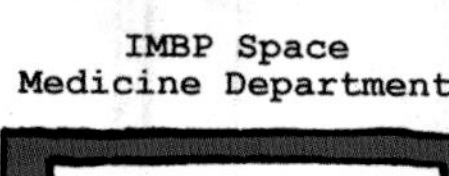
IMBP Space Medicine Department

General Staff Meeting ...
January, 1957
So, we must be ready. Lt. Col. Yazdovsky...?

Thank you, Academician Blagonravov.
Intensive animal training will continue ...

We have built a new engine vibration simulation chamber ... each dog will undergo sessions in this ...

Comrade Dubrovsky will, as ever, be in charge of dog-handling ...

She will be timetabling training schedules, so if you need to book an animal, please confer with her.
On to other business ...

So, the first thing on Yazdovsky's list was recognition of **Comrade Dubrovsky** in front of Boss Blagonravov **and** the whole department! A **commendation**.
I suppose so.

I'm sure you had something to do with it.
Oh, I make my observations but Yazdovsky forms his own opinions. He was showing how much he trusts you.

Dr. Yazdovsky trusted me to do a good job from day one.
As I recall, it was you who had to be won over!

Indeed. And we passed that point a long way back.

Come on, Yelena ... why so glum?
We live in exciting times, we have exciting work ...
I know ...

But when I heard about the new engine simulation chamber I began thinking about what the dogs will have to go through.

That's one of the reasons we train them – so they'll cope better.
Actually, seeing Blagonravov today reminded me that you once mentioned a story about him ...?
Oh, that ...
That would be about **Tsygan**.
Tsygan? A gypsy?

No, Tsygan was a dog.

Six years ago, Blagonravov attended the very first biological rocket launch, which contained two dogs, Tsygan and Dezik.

They were the first animals successfully recovered after a vertical flight to the edge of space ...

Unfortunately, on the next launch, Dezik was killed along with another dog when their parachute failed.

Blagonravov decided that Tsygan shouldn't have to fly again and took her home with him.

So **he** broke the golden rule! Don't get too emotionally attached.
Indeed.

RARF?
You see ...

WOF!
WARF?

...
ROWF!
WOF!
ROF!
ERF?
WOWF!
RARF!
WOF!
AROOO!
WOOF!

... it's impossible not to care about them.

I know these "street mutts" better than I know the **people** in this place.
Albina – the matriarch and space veteran, fussy, but protective of the others ...

I -
Rzhaya, the proud lady, Belka the joker ...

... Mukha the glutton who'll eat anything **but** gel space food ...

... dopey Dzyhoyna, darling Damka, wilful Modnitza ...

... and Kudryavka ...

... sweet-natured and empathic Kudryavka, so good at adapting her own moods to suit yours ...

She wants to please and to be loved. But she's very patient and determined, which is what gets her through the training.

A survivor.
Yes. I think that something traumatized her once.

What were you saying?

I was just saying ...

... try not to care too much.
Like Blagonravov?

Oleg Georgivitch ...

I'm sorry. It's good advice. I'll remember it.
Right. Yes. I'd better get on.

RRRF!

"Yelena!"
"Mistress Yelena!"

"It's **me**, Kudryavka!"

What d'you want, my little limonchik?

"I heard the story Oleg Georgivitch told you."

"We all did."

"Can't you take **me** home with **you?**"

No, take **me**.
Me!
No, **me!**
Me!

"No, she'd only take Kudryavka if she could. If she were **allowed**."

"We all know Kudryavka's her favorite."

"It's not true! She cares for all of us!"

Please, take us home!
Release us!
Me!
Me!
Me!
Please – me!
Take me!
No, me!
Me!
Me!
Me!
Me!
Me!
Me!
Me!
Sssh...
Be quiet.
It's me who gives you voice.
RRF?
But you can sense things, can't you?
SNF
"Good dog."

IMBP, Monday May 27th, 1957

Five months later

Comrade Dubrovsky ... Lt. Col Yazdovsky ...
We are very sorry that Rzhyaya and Dzhyoyna will not be returning to the kennels.

What happened?
I'm sorry ... that's confidential.

Of course.
But I can tell you it was a malfunction from which we gained valuable data.
The Chief Designer sends his regrets.

Tell the Chief Designer thank you. And will you ask him something for me, Boris?
Certainly.

Ask him when he's going to make one of those damned vehicles safe enough to carry a man!
Haha! So we don't have to risk any more dogs' lives?

I'll pass the message on.
Thank you. Goodbye, Boris.

Oh, well ... onward.
Konstantin, Yakov – clean out the empty cages, will you?
Yes, Comrade Dubrovsky.

You don't seem too ... troubled.
Should I be? The nature of this job doesn't really allow me that luxury, Dr. Yazdovsky.

I see. Dr. Gazenko once ventured to me that you might be upset if a dog were to fail to return.

Of course I feel a little sad. One gets to know these dogs. But I realize the importance of remaining as dispassionate as possible – we all do.

As I've observed. I think you're doing an excellent job.
...
Thank you, Doctor!

In fact, I'd like to get more of your input. Your insights into the dogs' behavior have often proved invaluable.

Perhaps you could submit written reports to me after each dog's training sessions?
Yes! ... Of course!

Call it a promotion, of sorts. I'll see to it that it's worth your while.
I – it already is! I enjoy the work and if I am serving my country in some small way ...

Comrade Dubrovsky – **Yelena** – you're a credit to the Space Medicine Department.

Good. That's settled, then.

... Thank you, Doctor!
Not at all.

Dr. Gazenko ...!
Hello, Yelena! Haven't seen you in a while.
How are you?
I don't know whether to be **angry** with you or to **thank** you!
... I'm **sorry?**
You told Dr. Yazdovsky that you thought I'd get **upset** if one of the dogs died!
Yes – **ages** ago – back when you first started!
And didn't I say to you, earlier this year, that we'd long passed the point where I thought that?
Yes, but I thought ... after ...
After what?
...
Let me collect myself.
I just wished to make the point that I take my job very seriously and wouldn't allow anything to get in the way.
I know that! **Everyone** here knows that –
especially me!
I also know how much you **care** about those pooches!

So I suppose you know that Rzyhaya and Dzyhoyna were **killed** on the latest "special flight"?

I hadn't heard that news yet, no.

Boris Chertok returned their traveling cages earlier.
He indicated that everyone at OKB-1 regretted the dogs' deaths and would do everything in their power to keep it from happening again.

I'm sure they **will** ...

Safety is the **biggest** issue. That's what our work here **and** at OKB-1 is all about.

But that's why we're sending up **dogs**, not **people**.

Don't patronize me! I **know** that!
I'm **not**.
I **never** patronize you.

Pff. Even the **Chief Designer** sent his regrets. **He** was **sad** when the dogs died!

I'm sure he **was** ...

... for about a **minute**.

What do you mean by that? He was extremely nice when I met him!

Yelena ...

He said he was **proud** of the dogs, of their big Russian hearts!

He's only interested in rockets.

Absolutely not. He was charming, he was –

Yelena, you've met him **once!**

That doesn't mean I wasn't able to get an **insight** into what he's **like.**

Be wary of him. He's a very difficult man to deal with.

I can't believe I'm **hearing** this! This, from **you!**

Yelena, Korolev is –

Korolev? Is that his name?

Dammit, I'm not supposed to reveal –

Korolev ...

Yelena, **listen** to me!

He was in a **gulag** – he's an egomaniac, a **bull** who stops at **nothing** to get what he wants –
Oleg! Be careful what you say!

A **gulag** ....! He's a **loyal Russian**, just like **us!**
Indeed.

It was during the purges ... there was no **crime**, as such ...

Nevertheless, he still hasn't yet been officially pardoned.

He didn't even join the communist party until very recently.

So what difference does **that** make? Are **you** a party member?
Besides, Khruschev **denounced** Stalin, his purges – and – and ...
... and I don't understand what you're trying to say!

Dammit, I'm trying to tell you that he says **anything** to get what he wants!

He's incredibly clever; he's an arch-manipulator, a **womanizer** ...
A moment ago you said he was only interested in rockets.

Dammit, I'm trying to tell you that he **JUST DOESN'T CARE!**
He's ruthless, cunning and he has very little respect for **people** ...
... let alone dumb mutts.
I **see**.
Perhaps we should agree not to discuss this any further.
Fine.
We'll make no further mention of it.
Fine.
Excuse me, Dr. Gazenko.
...
Yelena ...
Good night, Comrade Dubrovsky.
Mm.
'Night, Konstantin, Yakov.

RRF?

RRF

OKB-1 Rocket Design Bureau,
Monday June 3rd, 1957

From: the office of USSR Chief Military Procurator

Re:
Sergei Pavlovich Korolev

Meeting of the Military Collegium of the USSR Supreme Court,
April 18th 1957

All remaining charges against the above-named have been summarily dismissed, due to the lack of any crimes.

Chief Military Procurator

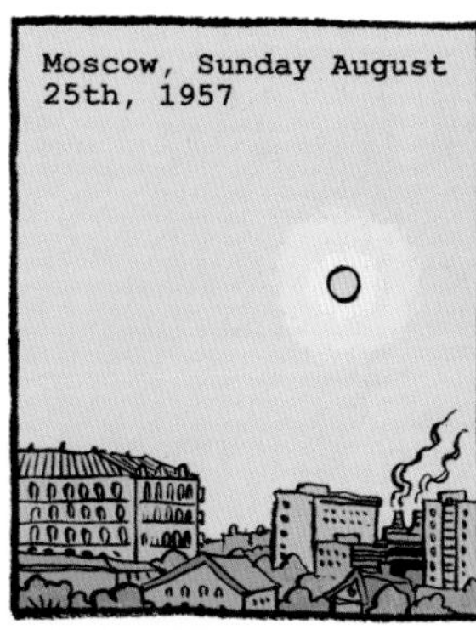
Moscow, Sunday August 25th, 1957

Gorky Park

Yelena, what's on your mind?

What?
You're thinking about work – *again*.

... Yes.

You've become so preoccupied since you've been there. Have you fallen for a colleague?
No!

Not unrequited love, then. Is it unwanted attention?

... *No!*

Mm. I can't think of many other reasons for such a long face! ...

Honestly! No job is worth it if it follows you out into a lovely, sunny day like this one.

IMBP, Tuesday 27th August, 1957
ARF!

Here we are, Cosmodogs ...
... happy landings!
Welcome home, Belka and Modnitza!

Yes, I'm pleased to see you, too!
But you've got to be patient a little while longer so that Doctors Parin and Seryapin can examine you ...
ROF!

Psst – Comrade Dubrovsky!
?
Yes, Boris?

There are no more "rocket dog" launches scheduled for about a year!

OKB–1 is busy with a host of **other** projects. ***Sssh*** – top **secret**.

Ha! I knew you'd be pleased.

Thanks, Boris. You're a dear man!
I try, I try!

I know what you're thinking.

Safe for a while.

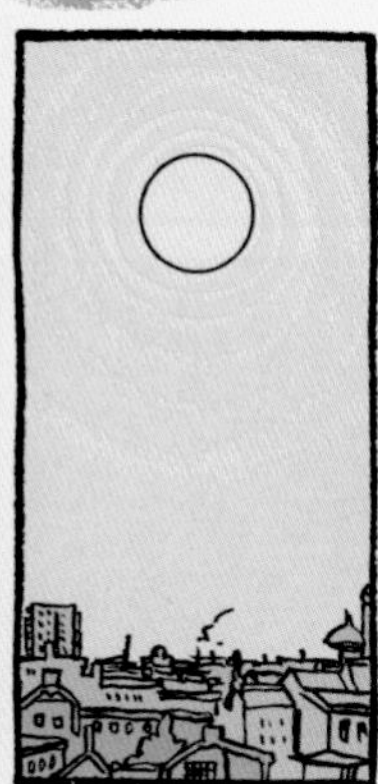

One must learn not to.
Every day, every moment
is a frontier to a country
that, once crossed, can never be returned to.

Most of the time,
we don't notice.

Which is just
how it should be.

The secret ...

... is not to worry.

You can't go back.

Although, those you leave behind ...

... will still think of you.

After all, something always comes along that changes *everything.*
And, once you realize this, you find that you're no longer *imprisoned* by this truth ...
... but freed by it.
I AM NOT A PRISONER ANYMORE!
I AM A MAN OF DESTINY!
THE LONDON TIMES
Edition Number 6,345,041 Saturday October 5th, 1957
USSR Launches Artificial Satellite
"Don't panic," says the Prime Minister. It's just a stunt by the 'Reds.'
La Planète Quotidienne
Les Russes l'ont fait. Ils ont atteint le rêve de l'homme de vol - le vol aux étoiles ! Au-dessus de nos têtes plane le nouvel artificiel par satellite, Sputnik 1, une balle en métal la taille d'une balle de plage. Cette machine a été envoyée dans l'orbite par la technologie Soviétique, un signe de leur superiorité
The DAILY REPORTE
Khruschev: The Soviet Premier on the USSR's Artificial Satellite
TIMES
A Chain of Red Moons: Beyond Khruschev's First Satellite
人是聲音
Die Welt Heute
Russen Schießen Raumschiff Ab!
Die UdSSR hat einen künstlichen Satelliten abgeschossen, ein Miniaturmond um die Größe von einem Fußball. Dies ist einer Welt erst und das Startfahrzeug wird sehr vielleicht von den Russen auf Deutscher Technologie basiert, die in den Nachwirkungen Zweiten
New York News
Only 2 cents! All the news you'll ever need!
RED MOON OVER THE U.S.A.
Chilling beeps have been heard coming from the sky. These are the sounds of 'Sputnik 1,' an artificial satellite launched yesterday by the
CONQUERORS OF SPACE
BEEEPBEEEPBEEEEEEEPBEEEEEEPBEEEEPBEEEEP

Saturday October 5th, 1957
Hello, you two. What's all the excitement?
Didn't you hear the broadcast this morning? The USSR has launched the world's first artificial satellite!
... What?
A Sputnik. We did it first! They say it's a validation of Marxism-Leninism ...
... A victory over capitalism!
Let me see that.
"An orbital satellite?"
But I thought we were only sending up ...
What?
Nothing ... nothing.
Beep-beep-beep-beep-beep-beep

Another, please, Kolya.
That's your third, Oleg Georgivitch.
I know.

Is it a woman?
Is it work? A rival?

Neither.

Both. And a dog, too.
Hahahahahaha! That's ***complicated.***

No.
It isn't. It doesn't ***have*** to be.

Thanks for the drink, Kolya.
Ignoring these things never helps, Oleg Georgivitch.

Indeed.
Thanks for the advice.

Same day
Academy of Sciences, Moscow
Emergency meeting of the Soviet Space Commissioners
Gentlemen ...

Premier Khruschev has sanctioned a **second** satellite launch ...
... we must be ambitious in order to sustain the success of this nascent space program.

... but it must coincide with the anniversary of the Revolution next month.
What?
That's crazy!
Yes.
There isn't much time to prepare, my friends. But we **must** keep our momentum.

The Premier has asked that we **top** our recent achievement. I proposed that the second Sputnik be a **genuine** orbital vehicle ...

... not just a satellite but a **spacecraft**.
The Premier **agreed**.

The second satellite will carry a **passenger**.

The second satellite will carry a **dog**.

God's Teeth!
A MONTH?!

I know. It's a crazy deadline.
Crazy? It's impossible!

And I just sent the whole bureau on vacation!

Call them back.

Vasili, we have the blessing of the Premier.

... We must make this date "without fail."

A month! Maybe it can be done.
That's the spirit! It's a challenge.

Now recall Chertok and the others.
We have work to do.

CHAPTER 4

IMBP, Monday October 7th, 1957

Oleg ...

I'm on my way to a meeting ...
I know – one I haven't been asked to attend.

It's senior staff only.
Something's going on.

I can't talk about it.
I know.

But whatever it is – I want to be a part of the team.

...
Please.

I'll talk to Yazdovsky.

Although I don't have any exact dates, I've been told we have a very short period of time to prepare three animal candidates for a new "special flight."

Dr. Parin, I'm putting you in charge of selecting these three. Two of the animals will be backups.

Dr. Gazenko will oversee an intensive training schedule for each candidate.

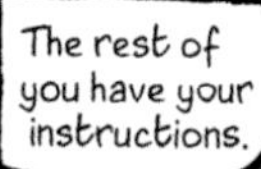
The rest of you have your instructions.
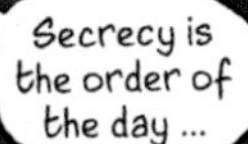
Secrecy is the order of the day ...

... never more so than *now.*
Remember, we're answerable to the **Chief Designer** ...

HA HA HA HA HA HA
... who will be here on Wednesday to inspect the candidates.

Let's get to work, comrades.

Vladimir? What about Dubrovsky? She knows the animals better than anyone.
Special instructions from above: senior staff only on this one.

Technically, she is a department head. She's dedicated, perceptive and conscientious ...
All right ...

... tell her she's on board and will assist you and me.
Thank you.

What kind of "special flight" is it?
I can't say. We'll all find out in due course.

Do we know which dogs have been selected?
That's up to Dr. Parin.

But I'll make some suggestions as to which ones I think suitable.

Oleg ...
Thank you.

Not at all, Comrade Dubrovsky.

"You fooled them all, didn't you?"

"Except Oleg Georgivitch. He knows how you feel."

Be quiet.

You agree, Dr. Seryapin?
Those three have proven to have the most even temperaments.

I was wondering if I might review the animals' names. I have some suggestions ...
I've *made* my selection. I was given this assignment, Dr. Gazenko. I wouldn't think to interfere with yours ...

Forgive me. I just thought it might help me put together the training schedule if I knew ...?
I will give the names to the Chief Designer next week. With his consultation, I will then select a final candidate.

Of course. Thank you, gentlemen.

...So we'll know Parin's choices then.
I've already block-booked the various training rooms. It's just a matter of slotting in which dog does what, when and where.

Efficient as ever, Comrade Dubrovsky.
Please stop calling me that.

Perhaps we should call this schedule "satellite dogs"?
Yelena ...! **Secrecy** ...!

Sorry.

"Good dog."
He's picked her, hasn't he?
I tried to get her taken off the shortlist.

I know you did.

Right, yes ...
I'll see you Wednesday morning.

I'll see you then.

IMBP, Wednesday
October 9th, 1957

1. Кудрявка
2. Албина
3. Мука

This means nothing.
I need to **see** the dogs.

Welcome, Chief Designer!

You remember our head animal technician, Yelena Dubrovsky ...?
Good to see you again, Comrade Dubrovsky.

Vladimir tells me you're doing a fine job looking after our dogs.
I do my best, Chief Designer.
Our dogs.

Now, Comrade Parin – the dogs you've chosen?
Yes. Ahem.

Mukha ...
Albina ...

Albina! An old friend – a good dog.

... and Kudryavka.
Of these three dogs –

Comrade Dubrovsky, will you have those three isolated? Just to be safe.
Immediately, Chief Designer.

... And keep them in smaller cages to further adapt them to cabin conditions.

WOW OW WOOF
ROW-OW WOW WOOF
Kudryavka! Ssh!

This one's feisty.
She's normally very placid.
WOF!

Dubrovsky?
It's true. Sorry, she's not normally like this.
WOWF OWF ROF!

Ssh! D'you want to be known for your **barking?**
WOWF

Ha! Yes!
That's what we'll call her!
WOWF ROF!

You see?
She's stopped.
She knows her name!
Her name?

Her new name.
"Barker."
Laika.

Albina and Mukha will be your backups ...

...LAIKA.

"Good dog."

Oh!
Are you all right?

Sorry – must've – it's been a long day.

For us all.
Chief Designer! I'm sorry – I thought you'd left.
The Chief Designer has requested a short time alone with the dogs.

Yes ... of course.

You moved your desk in here.

Temporarily. I can keep an eye on them better this way.

I admire your dedication.
Now, if I may ...?

Hello Albina ... Mukha.

And hello, **Laika**.
You know it's **you** I've really come to see.

I'm sorry that you're in that cage instead of running free. *I* was a prisoner once ...

I feel as though I've been in a cage for a long, long time.
Stalin's henchmen ... came in the night ...

They accused me of sabotaging research on missiles and rockets.

They accused me of wrecking my own life's work – and all on that lying bastard Glushko's say-so. The absurdity of it ...
Then, with no trial, no investigation ...
... no *voice* ...

... they sent me to *Hell*.

Hell is not fire.

Hell is **cold.**
Hell is a place that freezes hope to death.

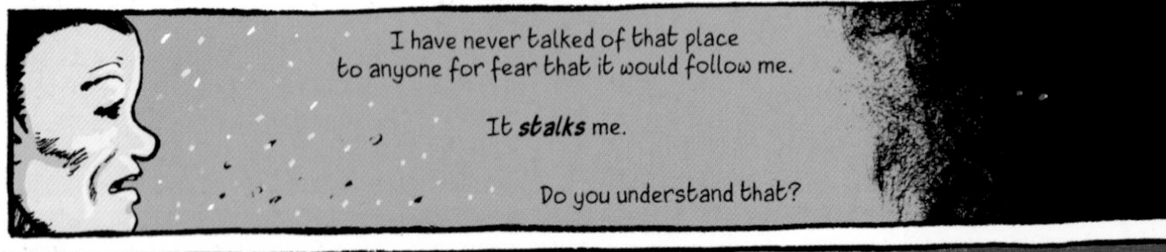
I have never talked of that place to anyone for fear that it would follow me.
It **stalks** me.
Do you understand that?

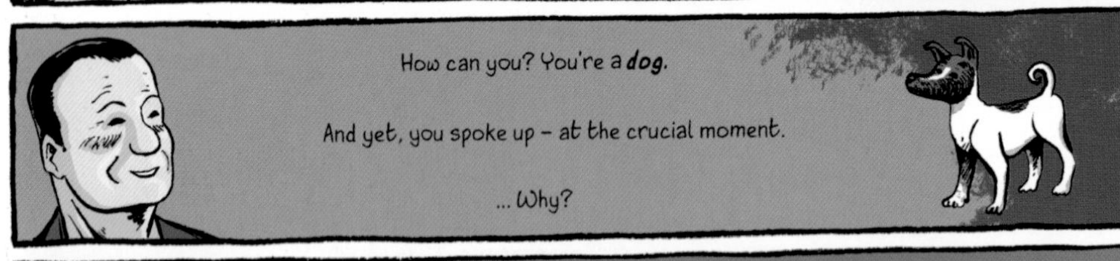
How can you? You're a **dog.**
And yet, you spoke up – at the crucial moment.
... Why?

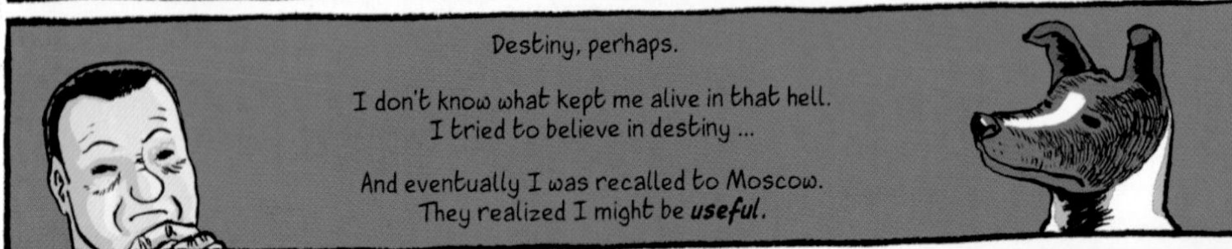
Destiny, perhaps.
I don't know what kept me alive in that hell. I tried to believe in destiny ...
And eventually I was recalled to Moscow. They realized I might be **useful.**

As I walked out of the gulag, I was starving. It was fifty degrees below freezing. I was delusional; it was as if an angel lit my way ...
I realized that soon I would surely die.
Do you know what saved me?
I heard the barking of a **dog.**

It led me to a loaf of bread, just lying there in the snow ... and then it led me to a warm bed.
I ate, I slept – and I *lived.*
A kind of miracle, perhaps.
I have learned *never* to ignore the barking of a dog.
You spoke to *me.*
For this, I will *honor* you. Everyone will know your name, Laika.
You know, those contemptible *scum* ... they did not overturn my original sentence until very recently.
My status was that of a paroled *criminal.*
Perhaps that's why I *still* feel like a prisoner.
So, for what I must do to you, I *apologize.* I *must* do this.
If I do succeed, then maybe I will finally be free.

And you will be, too.

You will fly further and longer and higher than any living being from this Earth ever has.

I am a man of destiny.

And you will be the most famous dog in history.

Has Dr. Yazdovsky gone?
He was called away. He asked if I'd look after you for a short while. Please, come this way ...

My **pleasure.**
Are you curious about all this, Comrade Dubrovsky – ***Yelena?***
Yes.

I have **many** questions, to be honest.
I understand. I'm in a privileged position. I can see what we're all working toward.

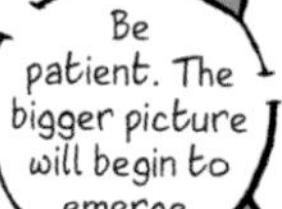
Information on this project is disseminated on a **need-to-know** basis. Even Dr. Yazdovsky knows only limited details.
Be patient. The bigger picture will begin to emerge.

Until then, I ask only that you continue to give such excellent care to our dogs.

I will. Of course.
But ...

But what?
No, I'm sorry, I shouldn't –
Please!

I –
I –
Can't you choose another dog?

Chief Designer ...
I would do ...
anything

No.
I'm sorry – it has to be this dog.

And now I'm more certain than ever that I have picked the right one ...

If Laika can so inspire you that you would risk everything to ask that question ...
Oh ... I ...

What have I *done?*
I'm sorry, Chief Designer ... I don't know what came over me ...

You *love* this dog, Comrade Dubrovsky. This is evident. You are trying to protect her from danger.

Believe me when I tell you that *I* love her, too. She is a special dog.
She is, yes.

Please, Chief Designer, I'm sorry if –

Ah, there you are.
Sorry about that. Had to attend to something ...

Vladimir, you'll need to bring the dogs over to OKB-1 next week for the test-fitting of certain items ...

Monday October 21st, 1957

OKB-1.
Ah, Vladimir!
And Doctor ...?

Gazenko.
Of course.
Dr. **Gazenko.**

Only two dogs today?
Mukha won't eat her gel food. It's nothing new – she's never liked it.

But there's no point in keeping her in the program if she won't eat.
True!

I knew I picked the right dog.

See how patient Laika is in her flight suit. Albina struggles, as always.

Gentlemen ... this will be Laika's vessel!
The first spacecraft ...
SPUTNIK II!

There are still problems, but we'll solve them. Even on such a tight schedule!
Why so tight?

Let's just say that the Premier has realized the propaganda value of satellite launches.

And he wants it up there as soon as possible?
Yes. We'll do it, even if we have to cut some corners.

This is Laika's container.
It's smaller than I thought it would be ...

The life support systems you lot at IMBP designed are inside, as well as heating, a camera ...
... everything to keep a dog happy.

Dr. Gazenko created the feeding system.
Valuable work, Dr. Gazenko, valuable work!

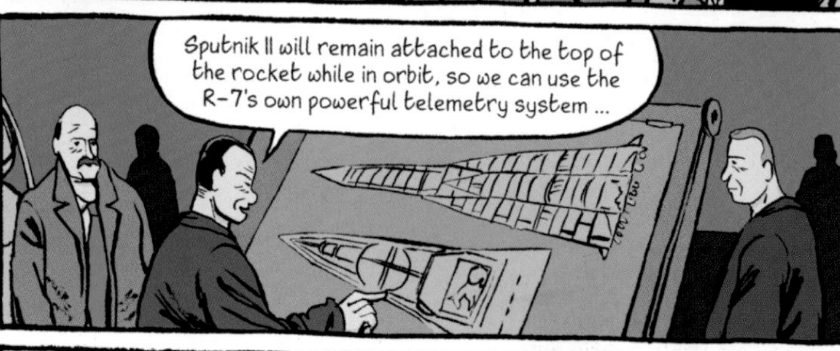
Sputnik II will remain attached to the top of the rocket while in orbit, so we can use the R-7's own powerful telemetry system ...

... Plus it will help dissipate heat, keeping the temperature in the dog cabin down.
And how will the satellite return to Earth?

It won't.

What?

There is no return option.
I thought you always try to get the dogs down safely!

Not this time. I promised Khruschev we'd do this in time for the anniversary of the Revolution.
Two weeks?
... A *tight* schedule!

So you see, there simply wasn't time to develop a return plan for the dog.
Right. One of the corners you cut.
Dr. Gazenko...

I promised Khruschev a dog would fly in space.
So Laika is a sacrificial passenger.
Dr. Gazenko!

Would you rather I sent a *man?*
Has anyone volunteered?
That's ENOUGH!

It's all right, Vladimir.
It *is* regrettable.

But I made the promise. What can I do? I have no choice.
Yes ... of course.

I ... er, the plan took me by *surprise*.

I *apologize* if I've given offense, Chief Designer. But I *had* to ask.

I respect you for that. I see why Vladimir sees you as such a valuable member of his staff.

I only hope that the technical achievement of Sputnik II will outweigh the sad but necessary sacrifice of one small dog.
Indeed.

Now, let's go over some dates.
The dogs will need to arrive at the launch ground on the 29th ...
And I must tell you about the radio broadcast ...

Excuse me for a moment, gentlemen.

... I'm sorry, Kudryavka.

I'm sorry, Yelena ...

Don't ever put me in a position like that again.
Don't take the Chief Designer on. He's powerful – and becoming ever more so.

I'm sorry, Vladimir. I was surprised.
We have to be matter-of-fact about this. You haven't formed an attachment to this damned dog, have you?

"Damned" indeed ...

Unbelievable! I was worried about Yelena going soft – we both were!

But all along I should've been watching you.

No.
There are people who care more for their animals than their fellow man. No – I – I'm a scientist.
But I favor good science.

Be careful what you say, Oleg Georgivitch, I can guess what you're getting at ...
... and as your boss and your friend, I'm warning you – keep your mouth shut. We're not here to question the purposes of our superiors.

Forgive me, Vladimir. I don't know what came over me.

Driver, let Dr. Gazenko off at the next corner, please.

When you return to work tomorrow, make sure you're the Gazenko I trust and rely on.
Understand?

Whew.

Dr. Yazdovsky! How did it go?
BOOMF!

...
Where's Dr. Gazenko? Is everything all right?

Gazenko was very ... **erratic** today.

He behaved inappropriately. He's suddenly got a case of the Blagonravovs!

I'm sure that whatever happened was a momentary lapse. Dr. Gazenko is a deeply honorable, loyal man.

Yes. Yes, he is, isn't he?

Before I forget, I need your help with something.
Some technicians are coming here tomorrow to record Laika.

There's going to be a radio broadcast. The Premier will introduce Laika to the people and the world.
ERF

Premier ... **Khruschev?**

Mm. Can you get her to bark on cue?
That's easy. Make her beg for food. It's really the only time she barks.

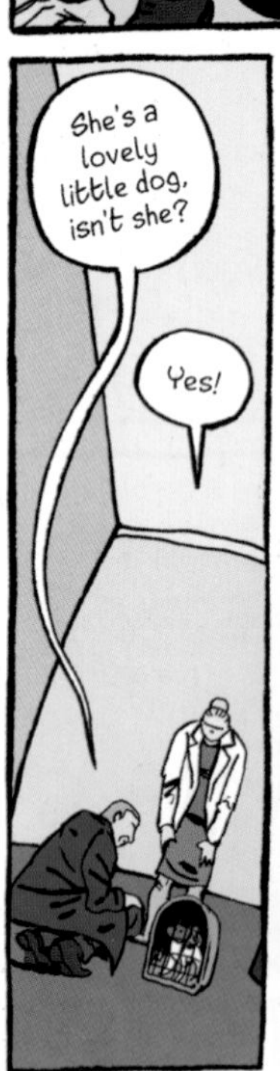
She's a lovely little dog, isn't she?
Yes!

No, don't let her out ...
Give me a pack of that gel food ... I'm taking her home with me, tonight.
... Home?

Yes.
Keep it quiet ...
I want to show her to my children ...

... let her play with them ...

... let her play like an ordinary little dog for once.

Doctor?
What's going on?

She only has a very short time to live, you see.
There's no return option on this "special flight."

She won't be coming back.
It's unfortunate. I'm sorry.

Don't stay too late.

Hello.

Hello.

You look like you haven't slept.

You too.

It's all right ...

I heard.
I know what's going to happen to Kudryavka.

Where **is** she?

Yazdovsky wanted to do something nice for her ... took her home to meet his children ...

Maybe you **got** to him, Oleg Georgivitch. Maybe it was **worth** the trouble you got yourself into yesterday.
You heard?

Not exactly. Yazdovsky alluded to an exchange.

You really don't like the Chief Designer, do you?

I understand why, now.

Oleg, I'm sorry for any misunderstandings we've had.

Doesn't matter.

Funny thing ... sometimes I fool myself that there are such high ideals in my work.
But it's all a **game.** And Korolev is the grand master of it.

Oleg, it's **dangerous** to say such things ...

Not to **you.**

Nevertheless ... I love my country and will do my duty.
That's all we have left, really, isn't it?
Yes ...
... maybe it is.
ERF!
Good morning, Vladimir.
... Good morning.
I apologize for my outburst yesterday. You can be sure that it'll never happen again.
Apology accepted. We'll say no more about it.
Would you take Laika back to Yelena for me?
You can trust me.
Good dog.

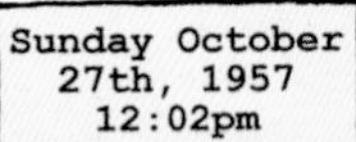
Sunday October 27th, 1957 12:02pm

The Americans have their own as-yet-unlaunched satellite, which they have named *Vanguard*.
But Soviet satellites are ahead - Soviet science is at the forefront of new technology ...

The people of the Soviet Union are building a new way of living!

The fortieth anniversary of the Revolution will be marked by the launch of a second artificial satellite.

This satellite will have a passenger - the first living creature to orbit this planet!
People of the Soviet Union, may I present to you ...

... LAIKA!
ARF!

ARF!
They're sending a dog up in a rocket?
I think that's what he means.

ARF!

ARF!

ARF! ARF!

IMBP, Monday October 28th, 1957 09.15am

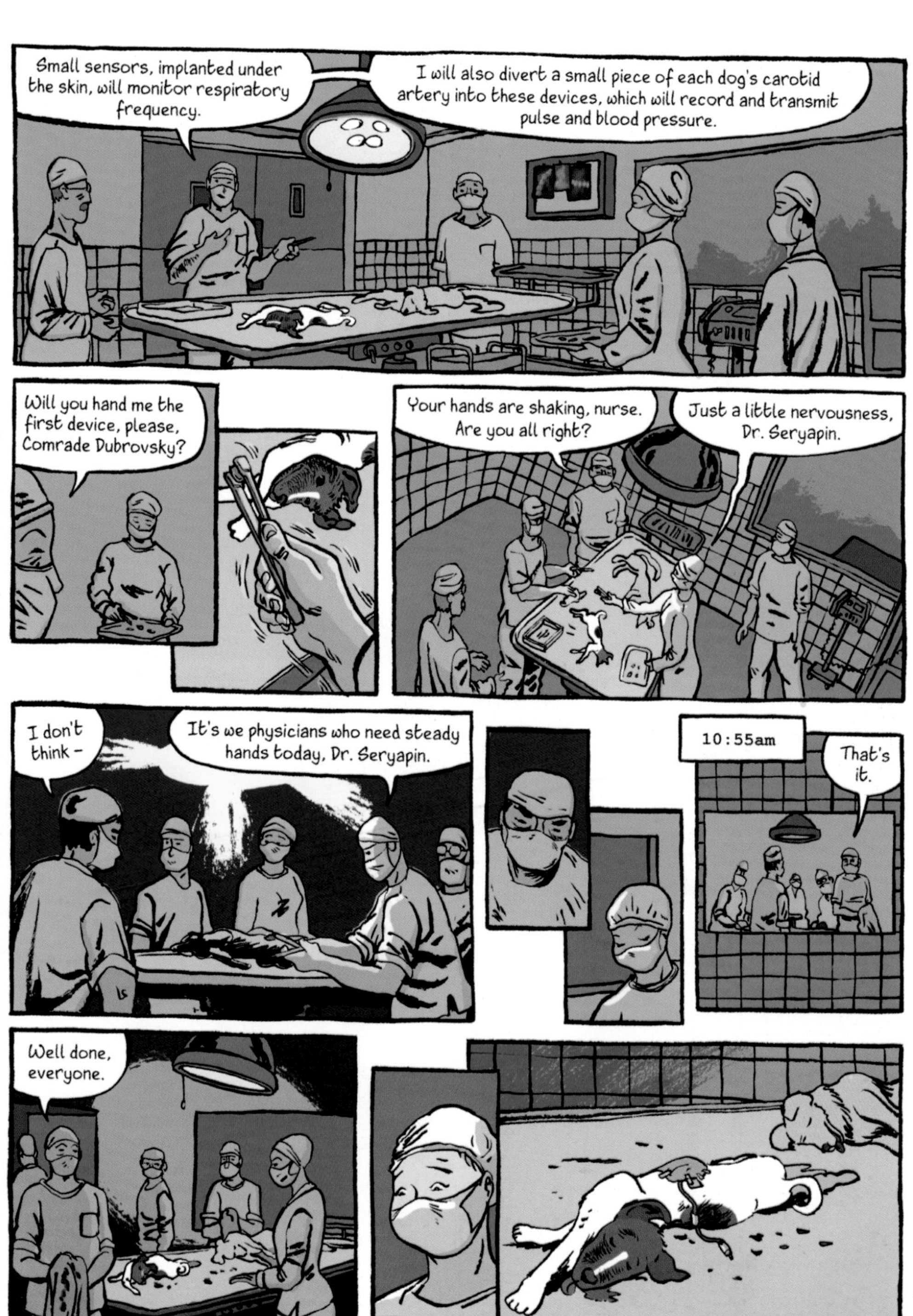
Small sensors, implanted under the skin, will monitor respiratory frequency.
I will also divert a small piece of each dog's carotid artery into these devices, which will record and transmit pulse and blood pressure.
Will you hand me the first device, please, Comrade Dubrovsky?
Your hands are shaking, nurse. Are you all right?
Just a little nervousness, Dr. Seryapin.
I don't think -
It's we physicians who need steady hands today, Dr. Seryapin.
10:55am
That's it.
Well done, everyone.

Tuesday October
29th, 1957
08:17am

Where's your traveling bag?

"Essential personnel only." I'm not going.
What d'you mean? You're overseeing the whole schedule!

The **training** schedule. Which is finished.

One of Yazdovsky's assistants at the launch ground **has** to be you: you're the dog handler. Our superiors have chosen Parin and Seryapin to be the others ...

This part of the process is theirs.
It's Korolev, isn't it? He doesn't like you.

The others don't answer back.
I can't **do** this ..

Yes, you **can.**
It's your **duty.**

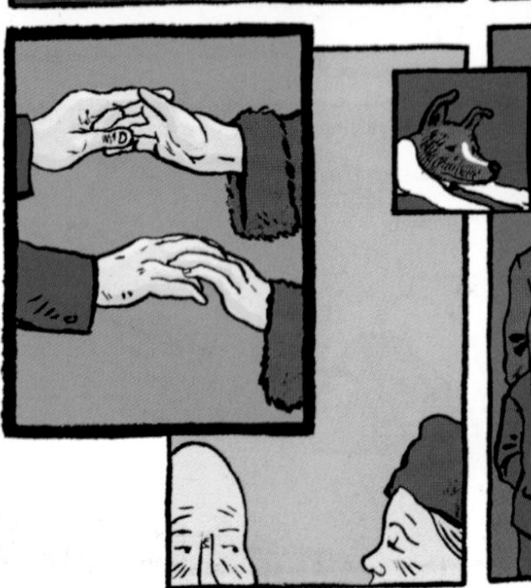

Are you all ready?

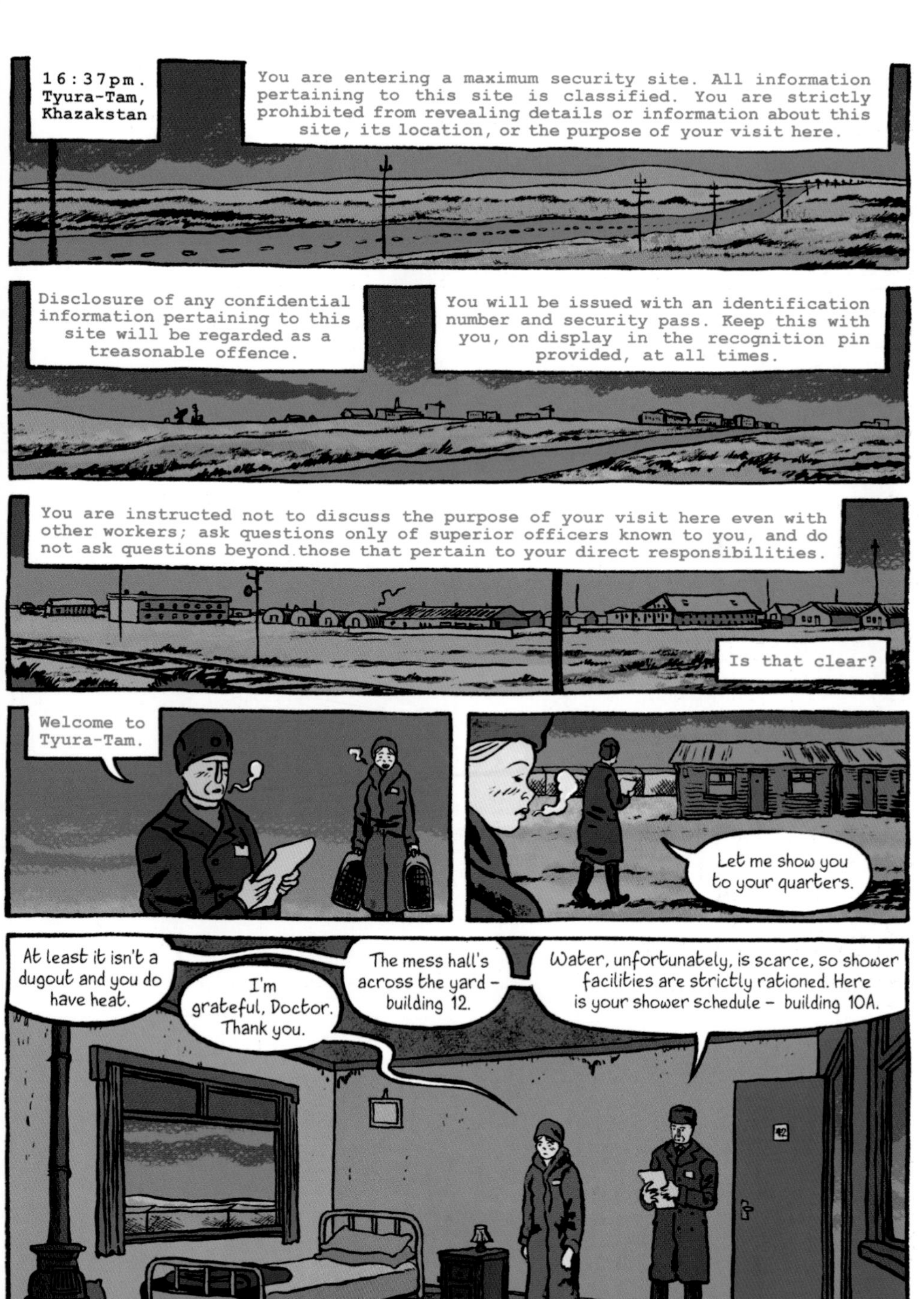
16:37pm. Tyura-Tam, Khazakstan
You are entering a maximum security site. All information pertaining to this site is classified. You are strictly prohibited from revealing details or information about this site, its location, or the purpose of your visit here.
Disclosure of any confidential information pertaining to this site will be regarded as a treasonable offence.
You will be issued with an identification number and security pass. Keep this with you, on display in the recognition pin provided, at all times.
You are instructed not to discuss the purpose of your visit here even with other workers; ask questions only of superior officers known to you, and do not ask questions beyond those that pertain to your direct responsibilities.
Is that clear?
Welcome to Tyura-Tam.
Let me show you to your quarters.
At least it isn't a dugout and you do have heat.
I'm grateful, Doctor. Thank you.
The mess hall's across the yard - building 12.
Water, unfortunately, is scarce, so shower facilities are strictly rationed. Here is your shower schedule - building 10A.
42

I'd be pleased if you'd join me and Doctors Seryapin and Parin for dinner tonight in the mess hall. Say 20:00 hours?

Thank you, Doctor. I'll be there.

Whew.

I thought you might be able to use these.

Thank you, Doctor!

Good night.
Good night.

Tyura-Tam, Wednesday October 30th, 1957

Four days before launch
05:58am

MMMMMM?

Are you thirsty?

07:27am

08:14am

10:00am

11:00am

12:01pm

ARF
Uh ...
Hello, Dr. Seryapin.

Do you see that over there on the horizon?

That's Site 1 – where they'll launch the rocket.

We're not supposed to discuss –
Or what? Yazdovsky'll have my head?

He's gone soft. Everyone's gone soft over that dog.

She has a ***name!***
RRRRR!

One that ***you*** don't call her by.

That is where they'll launch the rocket from. You can see it from your window.

It's a privilege to witness this, you know.

This is ***history*** being made!
They're stacking the rocket now ...

Tomorrow we'll have to put the dog inside –

17:15pm
Both in perfect health. All sensors functioning perfectly.

So ... you can go home, Albina.

Yelena, tomorrow we must transport Laika to the assembly building. I'll pick you up at 0800 hours.
I understand.

Come on, you two – stop playing around!
RARF

Come on, Albina. That's it. Good girl. Come on, Kudryavka.

19:11pm

What are we doing here?

Don't you worry about it.

No, really. What are we doing here?

This place is a freezing wasteland!
It smells strange, too.

It stinks of sweat!
Some man lived in this hut ...

... and he stank. You can smell what he felt ...

... and he didn't feel good.

The plane that brought us here reeked and this place stinks even more!
Yeah!

What a stench!
A barren, stinky –

Sssshh. Be quiet.

No, I won't be quiet. It's not fit for a dog ...
... much less you, Mistress Yelena!

HA HA HA HA HA HA

Oh, it's fit for me, all right ...

... and all my kind.

But it's not fit for you.

HA HA HA HA HA HA

Talking to dogs ...

I wonder ...
... how much do you really understand?

Anything at all ...?

Is it just the tone of my voice you respond to ...?

How do you seem to ***know?***

What is this place?

This place ...

... is a place where ***we*** do what we do best.

Where we don't let dogs be dogs ... or even people be people.

This place ...

... this place is a ***monument*** to man's ambitions.

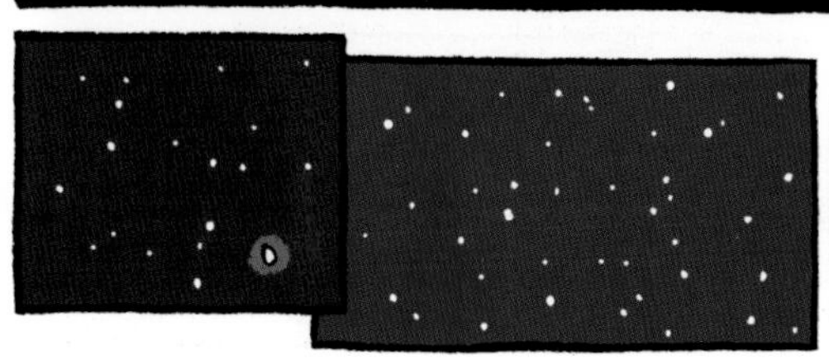

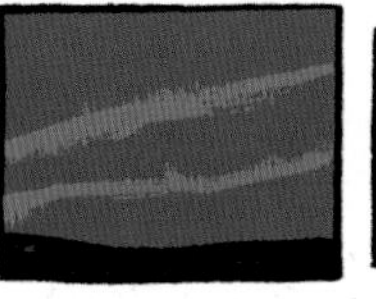

Thursday October 31st 1957, 08:11am

Yazdovsky ... Seryapin ... Parin ...

Please exchange your clothing for lab garments in there.

Is this the experimental animal?
Laika.

And you are ...?
Dubrovsky – animal technician. ***Dog handler.***

Do you have a scientific designation?
No.

I'm afraid you don't have clearance. You'll have to wait here.

I need her. She's part of my team.
It's procedure. Scientific and engineering personnel only.

Wait here, Yelena. I'll sort this out.

I need to take the animal and have it dressed in its flight suit.

I'm sorry – you've just told me to wait here and I can't release the dog to you until I'm told to by a senior officer whom I recognize. It's ***procedure.***

Very well.
Let's have a look at you ...

OW!
It *nipped* me!

What's going on here?

Chief Designer, I was just checking the animal. It needs to be suited up –
Idiot. That's what Dubrovsky's here for.

She doesn't have clearance –

SHE DOES NOW!

This way, Yelena.

Procedure is as follows: the dog must be washed in alcohol solution.

Good dog.

The dog must be dressed in the undervest.
Good dog.

The dog must be dressed in the sanitation suit.

The dog's harness must be attached.
Good dog.

Gentlemen - if I may?

Thank you, Yelena.

ARF?
Mistress Yelena?

My apologies for the misunderstanding about your clearance.
It's fine.

I imagine you must be quite angry with me.

No. I'm resigned to the situation. Some things you can change ...

... and some things are fated. Do you believe in destiny, Yelena?

You do.

I believe in it enough to know that even you must be at its mercy, Chief Designer.

Well put.

Please – let me be there for the launch ...?

Some of the workers here are superstitious. They think it's bad luck for women to be at launches.

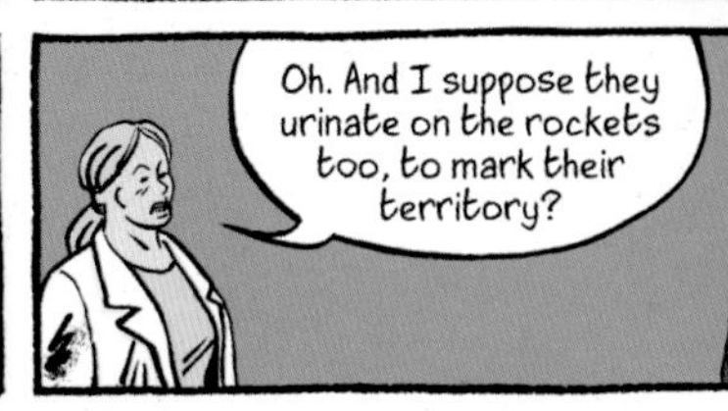
Oh. And I suppose they urinate on the rockets too, to mark their territory?

You possess shrewd insight into the workings of the male mind, Comrade Dubrovsky.

I've already arranged for you to have full security clearance. Here's your pass.

ARF!

Mistress Yelena!

Food delivery system check.
Air regeneration system check.
Check
There's been no time!
Camera system - check
Monitoring equipment - check.
Can you look at that waste collection system?
OK, let's lift this thing into place.
Mistress Yelena!
Midday October 31st 1957
That's it!
Just needs to be riveted into place ...
RRRRRR
RRRR
Experimental animal secure!
Satellite ready for stacking procedures!
ARF!
Mistress Yelena!
Mistress Yelena!
Yelena?
Yelena!
Wha -?
Oh!
I have a job for you.
Yes, Doctor?
Involving Laika.
Yes, Doctor.
Her compartment will soon be connected to the rocket and rolled out to the launch pad.
We can't seal her in until the rocket is fueled and its own systems check out on the pad.
So she'll need looking after.
She'll need to be kept warm.

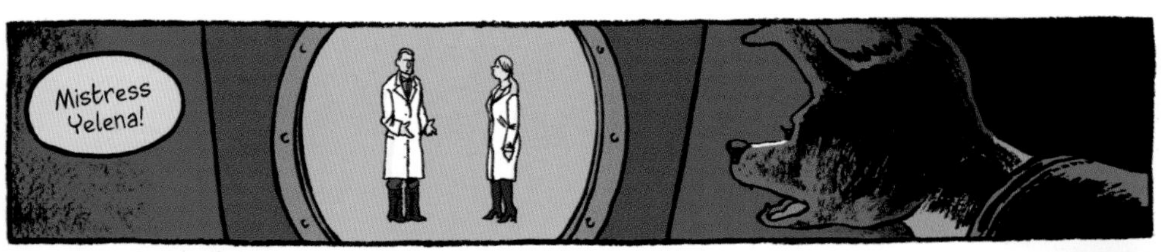
Mistress Yelena!

We're going to feed an air hose through her access porthole.

It'll pipe in warm air to keep her comfortable.

I don't understand. How long is it until launch?

Nearly three days.

I see. We don't want her dying of cold on the pad before she reaches space, do we?

I don't want to hear any talk like that – not in front of our colleagues from OKB-1.

Perhaps you're tired. I'll delegate this job to someone else.

I'm sorry, Doctor.
I didn't think –

Dr. Parin! Dr. Seryapin!
When the rocket is on the pad, you will keep a constant check on Laika.

And until launch, Comrade Dubrovsky, I suggest you return to your quarters. Get some rest.

Mistress Yelena!

I thought you said this dog didn't **bark** much ...?

Mistress Yelena!
Mistress Yelena!

Mistress Yelena!

Mistress Yelena!

Mistress Yelena!

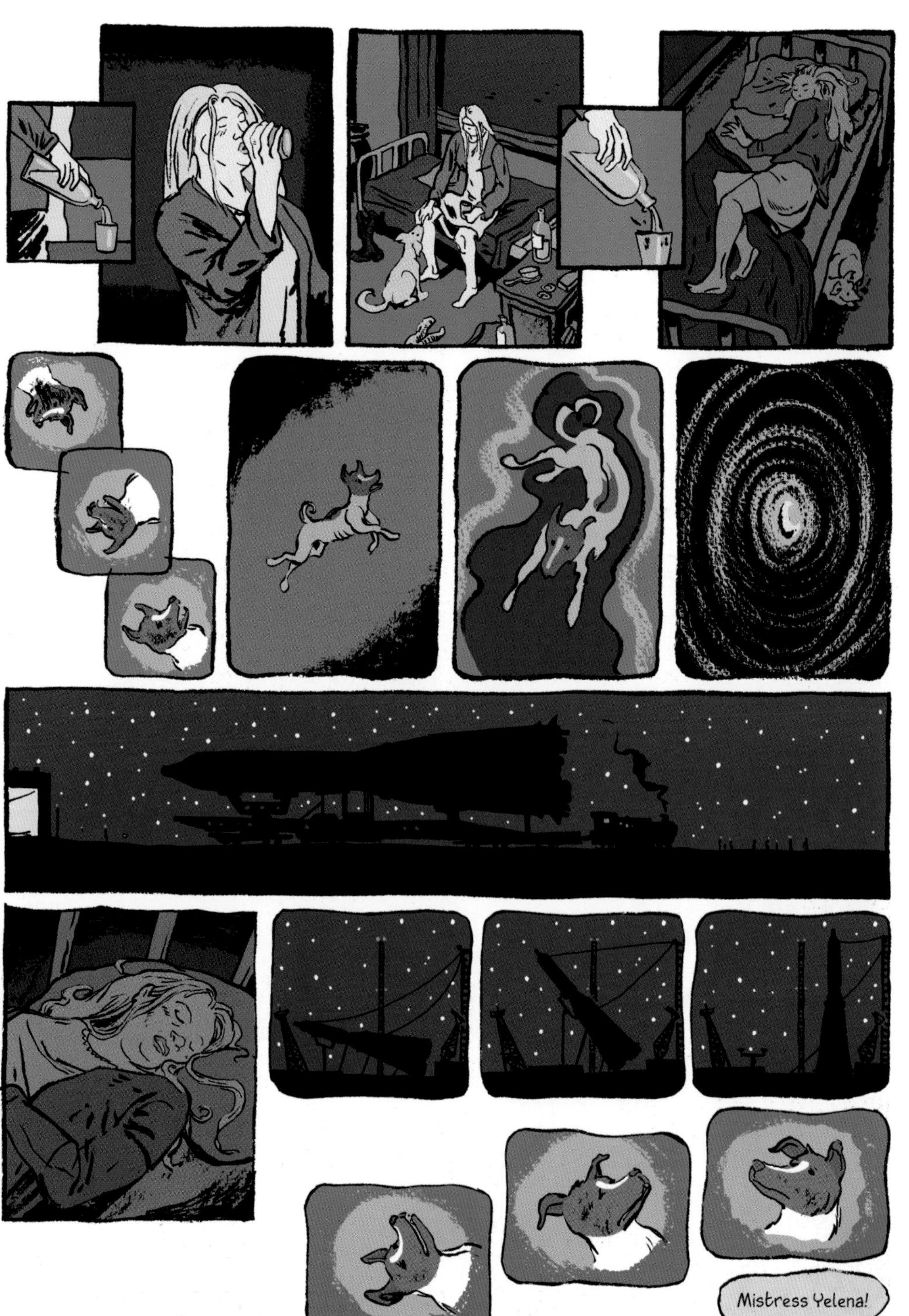
Mistress Yelena!

Kudryavka ...
RoF!
... Albina!

Friday November 1st, 1957

10:00am

13:00pm

17:00pm

18:30pm

19:30pm

Mistress Yelena!

It has to be this dog.
COMRADE DUBROVSKY!

Dubrovsky!

?
Hey, Dubrovsky!
NOK
NOK

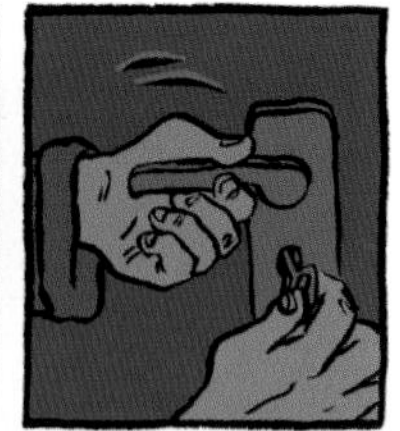

Dr. Seryapin!

Yazdovsky's asked that you and I do a final check on the dog.
He has?

Yes.
He says you can give it a drink.
Hurry up. The car's waiting.
42

Saturday November 2nd, 1957, 00:50am

Are you the other animal inspector?

What? Uh, yes ...

OK. Go on up.

WOF!

Hello, Kudryavka.
Mistress Yelena!

Oho. **Green light**.
Time to ***lock up***.
What are you doing?

Unplugging the warm air hose. They're switching the life support over to onboard systems.

It's time to seal the capsule.

Mistress Yelena?
Excuse us, please.

Farewell, Laika ... little Kudryavka.

Mistress Yelena!
Bolts fixed.
Container hermetically sealed.
RRRRRRRR

Check?
Check. Let's get this outer hatch sealed, too.

CLUNGGG

CHKK

Right, let's go.

Tell the command bunker we're ready for box room retraction and final preflight checks.

It's incredibly impressive, isn't it? Once you see it up close – the gantry, the rocket ...

... you begin to realize just what the Chief Designer has achieved.

I'll say it's impressive. That dog's going to be the world's first, genuine space traveler!

HAHA!
HAHA!

But it's a **special** dog, right, Comrade Dubrovsky ...?

Right, Dubrovsky ...?
Seriously ...

ОПАСНОСТЬ
... she'd **have** to be a special dog, don't you think?
!

Hey! **WAIT FOR ME!**
VROOM

Ha. Don't worry, Comrade Seryapin ...
... We'll drop you back at the barracks.

Mistress Yelena ...
Let me out ...
Can't you take me home with you?
Ohhh ...

Sunday November 3rd 1957

Launch Day
02:00am Moscow Time

02:15am

02:52am
NOK NOK

Are you ready?
Yes, Doctor.

Dr. Yazdovsky ...
Yes?

Thank you for allowing me to check on K – on Laika that last time. She enjoyed her drink of water.
That's all right.

I also wish to apologize for my conduct at the assembly building on Thursday.
No need, Yelena. We've all been under a lot of stress.

Now, shall we go? Before we freeze!
Yes, Doctor.

Launch Command Bunker, Site 1

03:25am

Stay here – I'm going to check on the medical telemetry.

How's the dog?
Blood pressure fine ... respiration deep.

I think she's asleep.

I wonder what she's dreaming about up there ...?
Dogs don't dream.
Of course they do. You ever seen one asleep? They dream about chasing rabbits. They twitch about, just like they're running ...
Rubbish. Dogs don't dream. They're just dogs!
"Just dogs."
"It's only a **dog**."
I must be **stupid**.
As stupid as the dog.
"Dogs don't dream."
Look!

Look, Kudryavka ...
... you can see the whole world from up here!
Isn't it beautiful?
Mistress Yelena?
Yelena ...?
Mmwha -?
It's time.
05:29am Moscow Time
Launch key to "GO" position.
Check - launch position GO.
IGNITION.

Good dog?

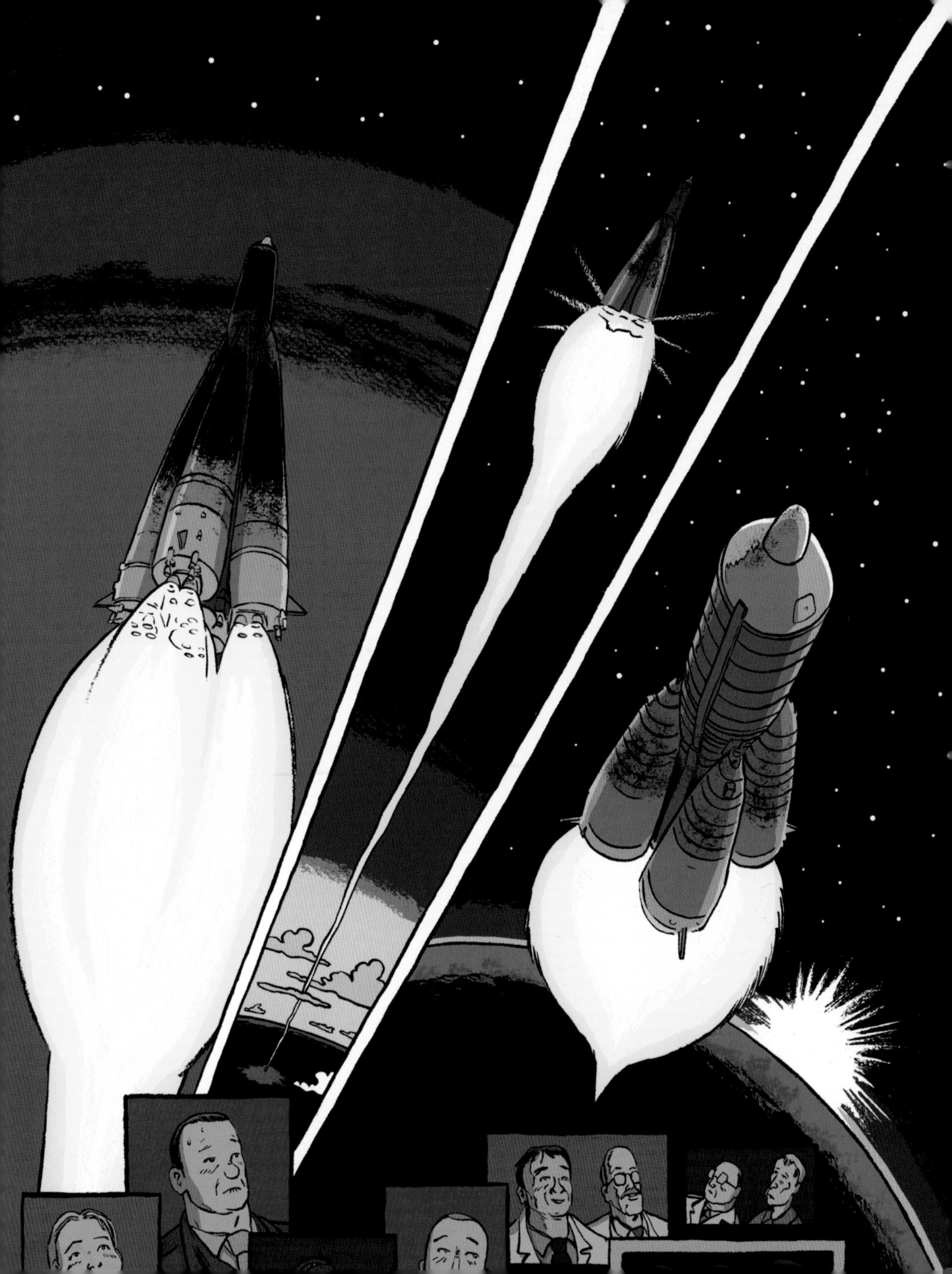

Look! ...
... Look, Kudryavka!

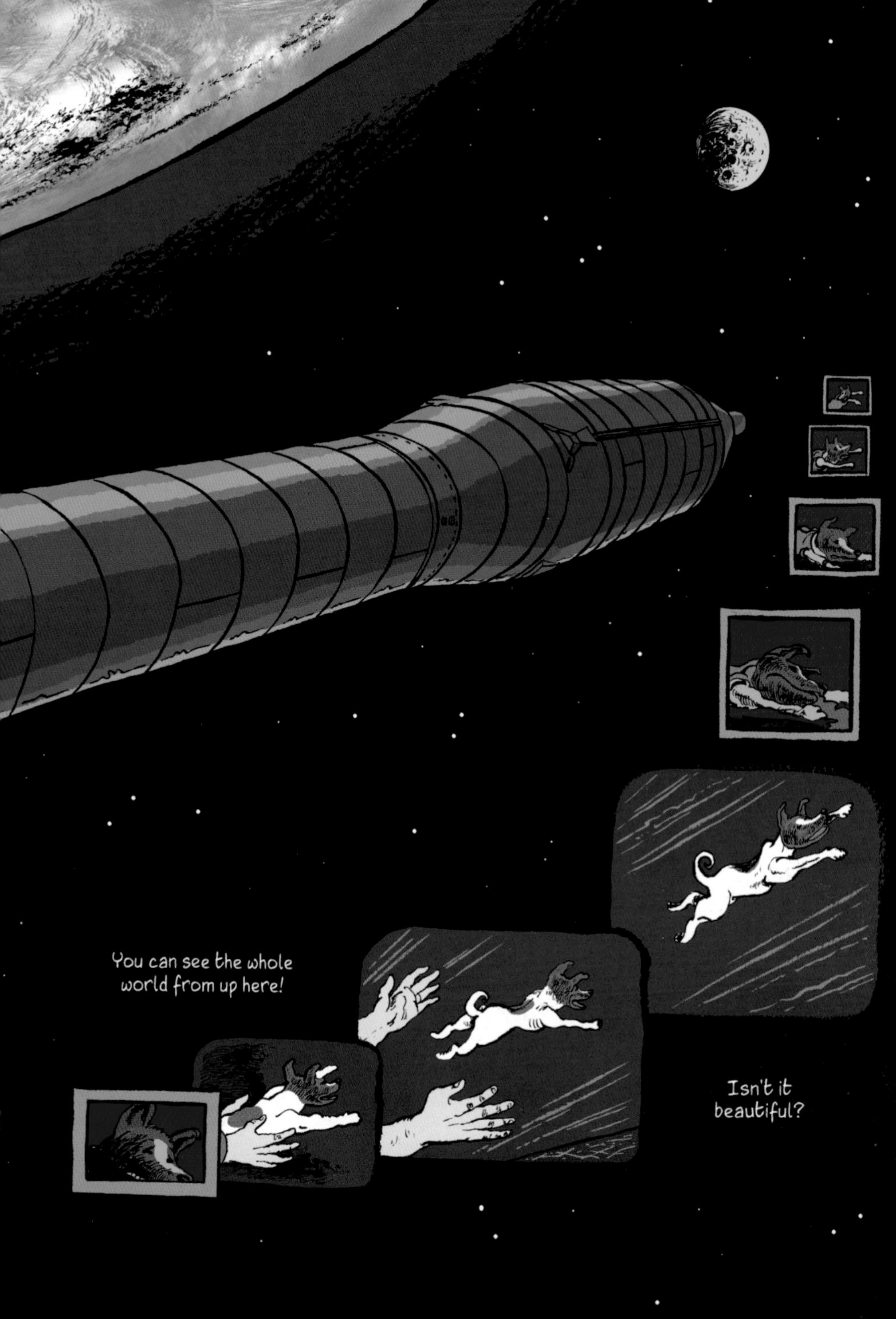
You can see the whole world from up here!
Isn't it beautiful?

Telemetry?
Experimental animal's pulse has tripled.

Respiration?
Nearly four times higher than prior to launch.
But, under the circumstances, vital signs are good.

She should be in zero-G, now.
Orbit insertion **successful**.

Yes! **WE'VE DONE IT!**
Ha! You've seized the high ground, Laika!

Orbit at inclination of 65.3 degrees to the equator. Velocity: 29,000 KPH.
Nose cone should've jettisoned ...

No, wait.
There seems to be a problem.

Well? Has it separated?
Unclear.

Might cause a problem with thermal control ...

Pulse rate beginning to decrease ...

But *slowly*. Only very slowly ...

She's panicking. She must be terrified.

Listen, everyone! Today we've made *history*.

Laika is alive! And if a dog can survive in orbit, then so can a man!
And a man will be next – you'll see!

Ryazansky, phone Moscow. Tell them ...

Tell them that Russia has successfully launched the world's first space traveler.
LAIKA!

Kudryavka.

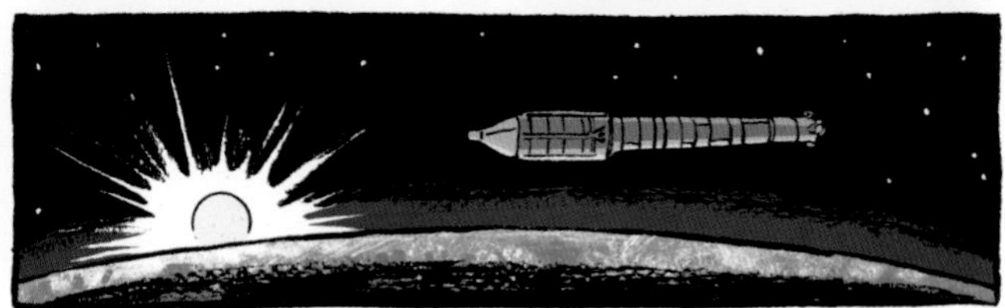

Mistress Yelena!

"Isn't it beautiful?"

"... we could be flying!"
"You can see everything ..."

"Everything."

07.12am Second Orbit
Satellite emerging from blind side of the planet now, Sir.
We have telemetry ...
TV signals?

Very faint.

She's moving.
Good dog ... **good** dog!

Something's wrong.

She's right. Temperature and humidity are rapidly increasing. It's getting very warm in there.

What's happening?
A malfunction ...? The nose cone, maybe. The heat should be dispersing.

...Third Orbit
... Not good. There's been a further significant rise in temperature in the dog's compartment.

She must be thirsty. She's eaten some of the gelatinized food – probably for the moisture content.

Body temperature's too high ...
TV signal?
Broken up ...
Shallow breathing ...

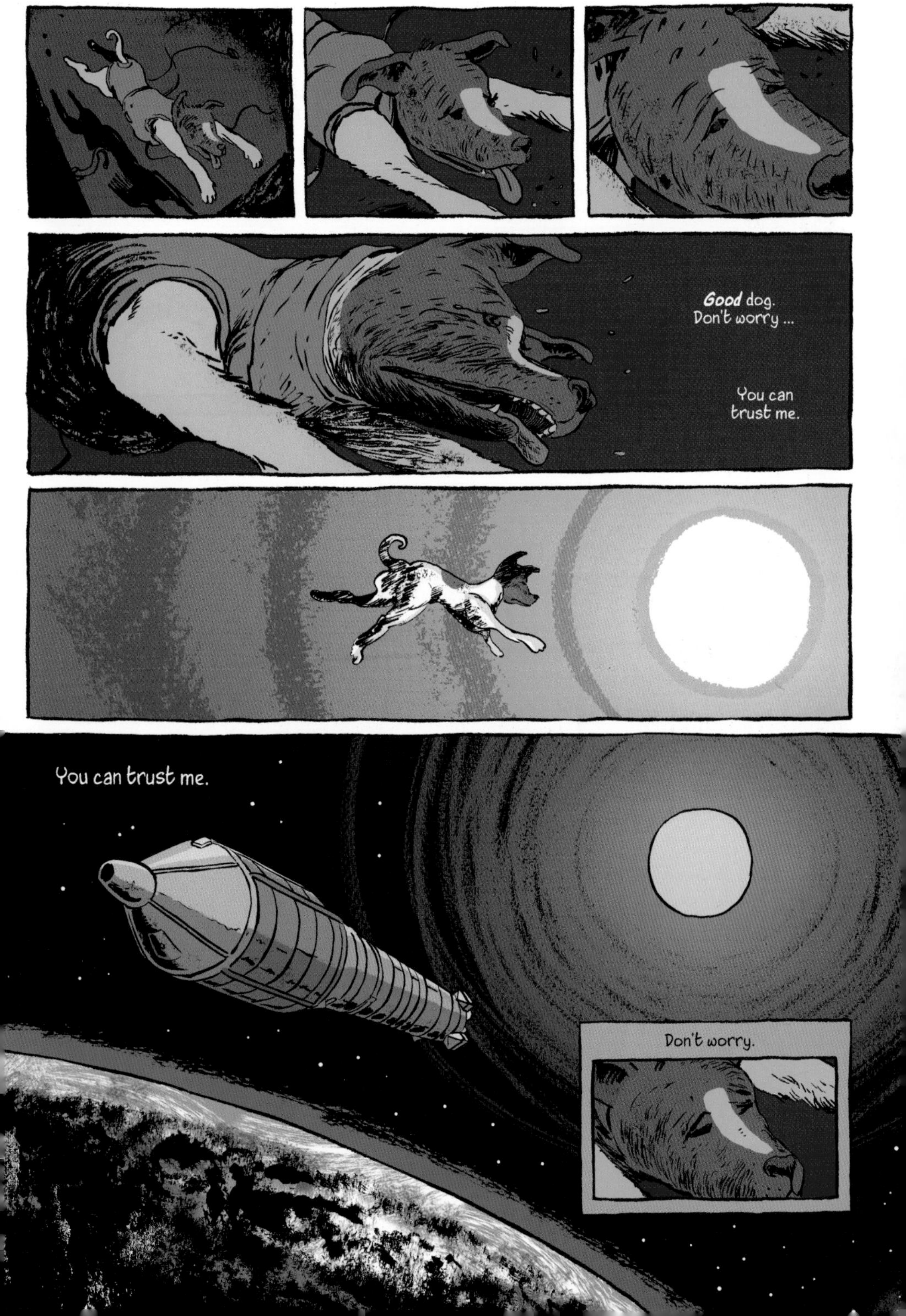

You can trust me.

Don't worry.

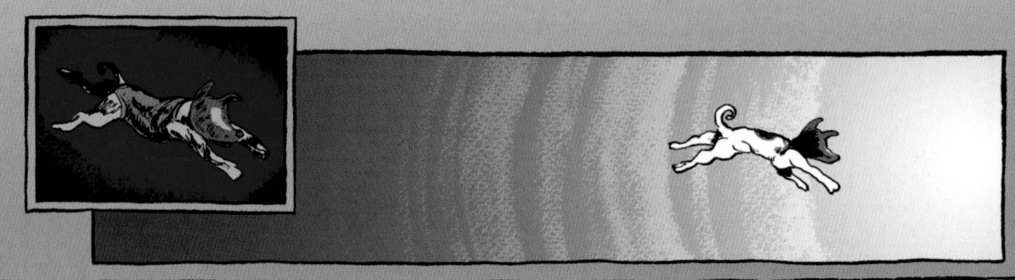

No one mentions this.
Not yet.
We'll wait and see what Moscow wants us to say.

Today at 05.30am, Soviet scientists successfully launched into space a second artificial satellite!

This achievement is dedicated to the 40th anniversary of the great October Revolution.

It is another feat of technological and engineering prowess by the Soviet Union!

On board Sputnik II is a living animal, the dog called *Laika* ...

... who is sealed inside a compartment with air and everything she needs to remain alive and well.

Her day-to-day activities continue as normal –

CLICK
A dog in the sky? I never heard such rubbish!

How can something stay up there, just going round and round?
Free-fall.

It's a scientific principle that –

Yes, well, I hope they get that dog down safe and sound, that's all.

New York News

Only 2 cents! All the news you'll ever need!

Edition Number 1,345,829 Monday November 4th 1957

Copyright New York Newspapers Ltd. A Daily Planet Company

SPUTNIK II LAUNCHED

Second Artificial Satellite Carries Living Cargo: a Dog Cal…

THE LONDON TIMES

Edition Number 4,446,007 Sunday October 4th, 1957 Special Edition

One Ha'penny

Second Soviet Satellite Launched

Dog On Board

La Planète Quotidienne

ANIMAL DANS L'ESPACE!

Comment les Soviétiques descendront-ils le chien

O M…

Lua … por …

人是聲音

我們的在俄羅斯的朋友在上面推出了一個第二紅玩具衛星進天空。蘇聯獨創性的這次第二展示包含一條狗, 更高比這個行星…

Die Welt Heute

Russen Schießen Zweiten Satelliten Ab

Hund ist Innere… Raumschi…

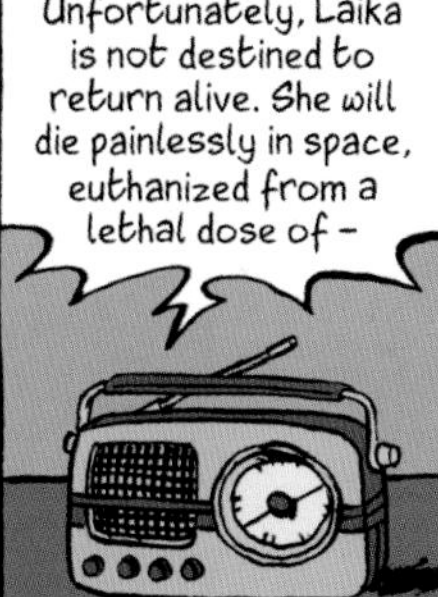

Lies.
Hello.
She survived for about five hours – into the fourth orbit.
I heard.
But the Chief Designer got the data he needed. And that's what counts.
That's what counts.
Oleg, my friends go to the park to try to see Sputnik II pass overhead.
They think there's still a little dog alive up there, in a bubble.
I know better, but I can't say anything.
None of us can.
I can't do this job any more.
I did my duty ...
I *did* it. But no more.
No more.

OKB-1 Rocket Design Bureau
"In London, a Russian embassy official told outraged dog lovers that many humans had volunteered to go into space aboard Sputnik II ...
"... but a dog was sent instead as the sacrifice of a man was unacceptable."

That one's from the London *Times*.
Ha! That official makes it sound like we've got a vehicle ***ready*** to take a man up!
But the world doesn't like that the dog died. It's terrible publicity!

The West seems as worried about the dog as they are about Russian superiority.
I doubt ***that***.

What's the matter with you, Boris?
We did something incredible. We built Sputnik II and put it up there in just ***one month!***

I told that poor girl at the kennels that there'd be no more dog launches this year.
Bah!
So what? It was a ***dog***. How could you have known that the Boss would convince the Premier to lob it up there?

Vasili! Come into my office, quickly!
Antonina's putting through a call from the Premier ...

Hello, Sir ...?
I'm glad you're pleased!
In spite of what the world thinks about the dog ...?
Good, good ...
Continue with the Object D satellite?
We'd be **delighted** to, Sir.
Yes ...
... we'll call it **Sputnik III.**
Thank **you,** Sir. Goodbye.

Khruschev **loves** us! It doesn't matter that the dog's lost ... it's all good propaganda to **him!**

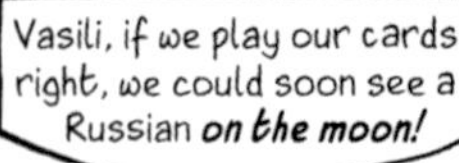
Vasili, if we play our cards right, we could soon see a Russian **on the moon!**

To the moon!
To the moon!

No, wait ...

To **Laika**.

To Laika.

Of course, **nothing** lasts.
Why worry about that?
The secret ...

... is **not** to worry.

Although, those you leave behind ...

... will still think of you.
We **still** think of you.

What will happen to it?

Sputnik II?
Orbital decay.

It'll burn up when it hits the atmosphere a few months from now.
Of course. **Sigh.**

It's strange. We Russians, we like heroic gestures, heroic deaths ...

In some ways, if it **had** been a man up there, perhaps everyone would have dealt with it better ...

... including **me**.

None of us, not even the Chief Designer, saw the backlash coming.

Actually, Vladimir, one of us *did* see it coming.

She *did*, didn't she?

And now she wants to move on.
Yelena wants to leave?

It'll be difficult to let her go. We'll have to extricate her from the whole program, re-evaluate her security status ...

Just transfer her. Her heart's not in the work anymore.

I should have listened to you back at the beginning ...

To Laika.
To *Kudryavka*.

To *Kudryavka*.

щенки!

Liliana! Milushka wants to go for her walk!
Coming, Mama.

Don't be long. Dinner's ready at seven.
Yes, Mama.

Hello, Miss Yelena!
Oh ...
Hello, Liliana ...

April 13th, 1958

"Work with animals
is a source of suffering to all of us.
We treat them like babies who cannot speak.

The more time passes,
the more I'm sorry about it.
We did not learn enough from the mission
to justify the death of the dog."

Oleg Georgivitch Gazenko, 1998

afterword

The Soviet Union stunned the world with the launch of *Sputnik 1*, the world's first artificial satellite, on October 4, 1957. Coming at the height of the Cold War, this bold statement of the country's technological prowess was a momentous move in the global chess game against the US – which would culminate exactly five years later with the Cuban missile crisis, that brought the world closer to nuclear war than ever before or since.

It is very hard today to imagine the atmosphere of these times. How could Nikita Khrushchev, the Soviet premier, decide that this dazzling success had to be followed up with yet another, in time for the 40th anniversary of the October Revolution (November 7, by the Western calendar)? That one-month timing was far too short, even for the brilliant minds running the USSR's space program, and it sealed Laika's fate by making her mission a one-way trip.

As the quote from Oleg Gazenko at the end of the book shows, the scientific value of *Sputnik 2* was minimal; it contributed little to the first manned space flight by Yuri Gagarin in April 1961. Even the propaganda hit was marred by an outcry over Laika having been sent to die in space. The official story at the time was that she had survived four days in orbit, when in fact stress and overheating in the capsule had killed her in less than five hours.

Nick Abadzis researched with impressive thoroughness—from the stacks of the British Library to Korolev's house in Moscow—all the facts that have come to light since the collapse of the Soviet Union. He then wove all available historical elements into an unforgettable narrative that achieves the power of myth. Cutting through the official deceit spread at the time, the story brings out the truly heroic dedication that these exceptional scientists showed, even as they lived in a climate of suspicion and fear. And Nick's imagination seamlessly filled out the personal stories, both canine and human, that bring Laika alive as a meditation on the meaning of destiny and the fragile beauty of trust.

– Alexis Siegel, 2007

BIBLIOGRAPHY

Books

Applebaum, Anne. *Gulag: A History.* 2003.

Békési, Lázló, and Török, György. *Soviet Uniforms and Militaria 1917 – 1991 in Colour Photographs.* 2000.

Dickson, Paul. *Sputnik—the Shock of the Century.* 2001.

Dubbs, Chris. *Space Dogs—Pioneers of Space Travel.* 2003.

Feifer, George. *The Red Files—Secrets from the Russian Archives.* 2000.

Golovanov, Yaroslav. *Korolev: Fakty i Mify* (in Russian). 1994

Harford, James. *Korolev: How One Man Masterminded the Soviet Drive to Beat America to the Moon.* 1997.

Semenov, Yuri P. *Rocket and Space Corporation Energia—the Legacy of S. P. Korolev.* Robert Godwin, ed., English edition. 2001.

Siddiqi, Asif. *Sputnik and the Soviet Space Challenge.* 2000.

Solomko, Y., ed. Memorial Museum of Cosmonautics brochure. N.d.

Video

Smithsonian Videohistory Program. *Soviet Space Medicine.* Interviews with Oleg Gazenko, Evgenii Shepelev, and Abraham Genin about their participation in the Soviet aviation and space medicine program. Interviews by Cathleen S. Lewis, translated by Andreas Tarnberg. (RU 95521). 1989.

Internet Sources

AllRefer.com: Soviet Union
http://reference.allrefer.com/country-guide-study/soviet-union/

Grahn, Sven. *Sputnik 2—More News from Distant History*
http://www.svengrahn.pp.se/histind/Sputnik2/sputnik2more.html

------. *Sputnik 2—Was It Really Built in Less then a Month?*
http://www.svengrahn.pp.se/histind/Sputnik2/Sputnik2.htm

Jorden, William J. "Soviet Fires Earth Satellite into Space?" *New York Times,* October 5, 1957.
http://www.nytimes.com/partners/aol/special/sputnik/sput-01.html

Korolev, Sergei P. *Synopsis of Report on Development of Conceptual Design of an Artificial Earth Satellite.* (Technical Plan for Object D Satellite for U.S.S.R. Government Officials). 1956
http://www.hq.nasa.gov/office/pao/History/sputnik/russ3.html

LePage, Andrew J. *Sputnik 2: The First Animal in Orbit.*
http://www.seds.org/spaceviews/9711/index.html

NASA. *Sputnik 2.*
http://nssdc.gsfc.nasa.gov/nmc/tmp/1957-002A.html

Siddiqi, Asif. *Korolev, Sputnik, and the International Geophysical Year.*
http://inventors.about.com

S. P. Korolev Rocket and Space Corporation Energia.
http://www.energia.ru/English/

The Story of Laika.
http://www.moscowanimals.org/laika.html

Zak, Anatoly. *RussianSpaceWeb.com*
http://www.russianspaceweb.com/index.html

AUTHOR'S NOTE:

In this book, all phases of the moon depicted on specific dates are accurate to the day—although I may have erred on the side of drama about the time of moonrises. So thanks to Paul Carlisle for his very useful online "Moon Phases Calendar." http://www.paulcarlisle.net.old/MoonCalendar.html

For Pierre Alexander Abadzis

1925 - 2003

Acknowledgements

Thank You

For assistance and advice in technical and research matters:

Kelly Crawford, Mykola Krasnokutsky, Al Muell, Katya Rogatchevskaia, Asif Siddiqi, Dave Sutton, Charles P. Vick and Anatoly Zak.

For all the support, help and inspiration:

Jessica Abel, The Aggs Family, Greg Bennett, Nick Bertozzi, The Bentley Family, Alan Cowsill, Gina Gagliano, Siobhan Gallagher, Rob Green, Myla Goldberg, Kat Kopit, Jason Little, Matt Madden, Steve Marchant, Tanya McKinnon, Danica Novgorodoff, Charlie Orr, Paul Peart-Smith, Juliet Penney, Chris Pitzer, Masha Rudina, Caspar Sewell, Mark Siegel, Xenia Sinclair-Murray, Hilary Sycamore, John West, Sally Willis and all my wonderful friends at Eaglemoss.

Special thanks to Jim Green and the Abadzis Family (especially Angela and Nadia).

If I've forgotten anyone, my apologies and please write your name in here:

Mention and thanks must also be made to (living composers only):
John Barry, Brian Eno, Neil Hannon, Joe Hisaishi, Bear McCreary and Thomas Newman, to whose music much of this book was drawn.

Please visit:

www.nickabadzis.com

http://www.moscowanimals.org

http://www.russianspaceweb.com

http://www.jimbus.co.uk/